# JIM AND THE RETURN OF SECANDRA BONES

DEEPANSHI YADAV

This is a fantasy book which is wholly devoted to the e-readers who possess the enthusiasm & inquisitiveness of rolling their eyes over pages filled with sorcery and occult.

A world of occults cannot exist in reality according to the boffins as there is no such thing as magic according to them which is undoubtedly true in some cases else than the times when people witness supernatural incidents or when they undergo thaumaturgy purported by a thaumaturgist. It could not be said whether magic is be extant or not but it could certainly be told whether there are bibliophiles across the globe who possess the inquisitiveness of reading fictional books, as definitely there are several of them.

After having a happy reading, your mind would patently develop a peculiar curiosity of 'What would be next ?' And this would only happen if you would get all the stuff written inside down into your mind without letting a single thought like 'How's this even possible ?' to emerge from any corner of your sharp brain which has an ordinary wont of judging things earlier than it actually get to know them.

"Whether you've faith in supernatural stuff or not but never believe on somebody's words very simply." Said by the author !

# Contents

# Foreword

*The book 'Jim And The Return Of Secandra Bones' involves the escapades of a twelve-year old boy and his best friends in a magical world which they mistakenly discovered while on their way in a dense woods , the children were unaware of the fact that they had set about onto an expedition of occults. The peers made it to the world in an adventurous way but they had not envisaged about being there for the rest of their lives.*

*In their past the children had suffered a lot, especially the main character but as they set their feet into the world, it seemed like all of their torments began to fade away until the main character had a very uncanny nightmare although it dwindled away from his memory slightly as he got the opportunity of getting himself along with his best friends admitted into the magical school of the mythical world.*

*Very soon the story took a jerking turn when the main character's girl-best friend befriended herself with an unusual (according to the main character) person who somewhat was peculiar in accordance of that person's behaviour. It seemed like that person befriended with the main characters' girl-best friend just in order to gain something from her, what would that be ?*

*The story revolved around the main character and his buddies' mischiefs until a new character entered into the best friends' privacy, who would that be ? The buddies allowed that person to make it into their amity, at their first meeting the children let that individual to invade into their lives considering that person to be amiable which indeed that person was.*

*As soon as the children let that person invade into their friendship, they found a very appalling thing off his/her mouth at the end of the story.*

# Preface

*This book indeed deals with magic, magic and only magic.*

*It is to be written so as to quench the thirst of the bibliophiles who possess the enthusiasm of burrying their heads along with their minds into mythical books without even throwing a single jiff of theirs into the bin by allowing their eyes to sight a book of any other genre. It is only written in order to cherish the people who does/does not believe on supernatural things.*

# Prologue

*The Characters' Names :*

- *Main Character - Jim Sueruds Other Characters - Sam Mahongthan Eveline Guitonnet Dorothy Jones Ason Adolpher Nadia Shimper Clark Watson Masarah Supie (Ro) Jack Faulter Kevin Bangthom Gilberd Sarah Bones The Devil Tulip Albatross Adrien Monton Naomi Fillurs Adam Se Johnson*

# CHAPTER ONE

# DOROTHY'S WARNING

"Jim ! Wakeup ! It's already half past eight ! Wakeup !" The boy with dark blue hairs woke with a startle and started moving his hands over his hairs to tidy them up. His blue eyes still seemed to be sleepy but he resisted his temptation and said calmly "Sam , why you woke me up ? It's not even 9." The boy with curly grey hairs shouted "Have you forgotten, the timing has been changed ?! It's not 9 now , it is 8 !" Jim felt a sensation full of fear to run down his spine and asked shockingly " What ! But how ?" Sam's brownish lips were trembling , he couldn't speak a single word but finally spoke out after a minute or two "How can you forget ? We three had seen the noticeboard along with a brand new notice yesterday that the timing has been changed due to the approaching summer !" Jim said furiously "Oh ! Yeah ! Now I remembered , how can I forget such a significant stuff ?!" He punched his face with his fist while speaking , then suddenly he recalled something and asked "What about Eve ? Did you wake her up too ?" Sam's face turned pale but he didn't say anything , he only spoke out when his buddy asked him the same question a trillion times. He told him that she had already left for class , Jim felt another sensation to run down his spine but this wasn't of fear but was of grief and sorrow that why they both argued with her yesterday evening ?! If they hadn't done so then they might've been in the class with their bestie.

After critically thinking quite a lot that whether they should head off to the class , finally at 8:45 Jim came up with a conclusion and said "Ah.. I think we should go." Sam who was till now getting annoyed after looking at his left leg's torn shoe constantly, turned his head towards Jim sharply that he felt a pain at the back of his neck, he asked in a shivering voice that what he was talking about. His buddy looked at him with sorrow and replied "We should head off for class." Sam was taken aback by his best buddy's words , he didn't had guts or even clear voice to respond but spoke out with a bit of anger in his voice " How can you say ..so simply ?! You know that if we'll do that , then what that ugly witch's gonna do to us , she will- she'll spare us into pieces for sure !" Jim shouted "But if we won't then it would mean we're afraid of her and WE AREN'T ..and also don't you remember what she had said to us on that day ?! THAT WARNING OF HERS !" Sam got a glimpse of Friday on which that ugly witch had warned them that if they would bunk one more class of hers then she wouldn't just give them toilets to clean but also both of them had to take off their robes in front of all the classes ! How much embarrassing and disgusting it would be ! NO THEY SHOULD HEAD OFF TO HER CLASS AS FAST AS THEY COULD ! These all thoughts were worrying Sam and Jim , finally Sam agreed to go. They both dressed up in a hurry, it was already 8:50 ..only 10 minutes were left for the ugly witch's class to end. From the ugly witch they referred to Dorothy Jones – Their language teacher- A young but very fat lady with short, curly black hairs, medium in height, fat palms , fat feet & always wearing a dozen of weird rings in her chubby fingers. They both rushed downstairs and began running towards her classroom followed by the eighth, first and fourth classrooms and at last they had reached – They both were standing at the door, pushed it and closed it but when they turned their heads ..they saw the ugly witch standing in front of them, glaring at them with red eyes just like an angry bull ready to attack. She roared "Fourth time !" She looked at the class and again roared "Fourth time these boys have come late !" She turned towards the two boys and asked ridiculously "What excuses d'you have this time ?!" Sam was about to open his mouth and tell her that they both had eaten a lot yesterday that is why their tummies had gone crazy but when he heard her saying that, he closed his mouth automatically. She looked at the class and then looked straight at a dark-black haired girl; ordered her to stand up, she did so as her teacher had instructed her to. "Why are you quiet, profitable bookworm ? You should have come up with something, by now. Are you not going to defend your boyfriends ?" "NO" The girl replied sharply. Jim looked at her , her eyes were shining with tears. Miss Jones said in a very different tone like it was unbelievable to her. "Oh really ? Then I think there's no one else who's left to defend ..you boys." She said while turning her face from that girl to Jim and Sam.

The whole class was listening attentively to their conversation and there was utter silence in the classroom, not a single voice was there else than Miss Jones' hoarse voice. The ugly witch then spoke out with a big smirk on her face "So, as I had warned on Friday ..that if you'll miss another class of mine then you'll be needed to.." She looked at the class and then said "Well , children. We're gonna have some fun.. OH ! Sorry my bad ,not some fun but .. TOO MUCH FUN !" She looked at a blonde haired boy- Ason Adolpher and a purple haired girl- Nadia Shimper – Her favourite students of all time who always informed her about every single move of the three best buddies – Jim, Sam and Eveline. They both smirked at her, the ugly witch asked the two boys in the sweetest voice of hers "So..what're you waiting for ..my sweeties ? D'you need any help ?" Jim and Sam turned up their faces to face her, their eyes had gone dark red due to anger. Again she asked "Oh my boys.. Do you want any help ? Well I don't suppose so. So go on, the entire class is waiting eagerly, you can't keep them waiting and not me either." Sam looked at his bro but he didn't look back at him instead he kept looking at the ugly witch. Jim moved his trembling hands towards his shirt, Sam couldn't believe his eyes- Was Jim actually doing that ?! Was he really going to take off his clothes ?! Was he actually obeying the ugly witch's mouth ?! NO JIM CAN'T AND HE WON'T !-Sam told himself but Jim was actually doing the opposite of what Sam was hoping for, all the boys were looking at him but the girls had shut their eyes except for Eveline and Nadia. Jim took off his tie at first which was quite easy to do so this time other than most of the times when he felt like he's gonna kill himself, then his hands moved a little lower and reached his first button. His hands were still shaking but his dark red eyes looked straight into the ugly witch's evil eyes. He unbuttoned his first button then his hands moved a bit lower again & he unbuttoned second button of his shirt , when he moved his hands a little lower to open his third button.. as he was about to unbutton it too then suddenly-"Excuse me Ma'am !" The girl with straight jet-black hairs called out loud to Miss Jones. All the students jumped and looked at her with anger as she had ruined an enthusiastic drama going on, miss Jones turned towards her and asked loudly "What happened ?" Jim looked at her, his third button still buttoned. "Ma'am I think you had warned them for bunking your class but they were late instead and therefore they're not needed to do any ridiculous sort of stuff like that." She told Miss Jones politely but confidently , miss Jones who had entirely forgotten what was the warning, shouted furiously "NO IT WAS NOT THAT !" "But ma'am it was it." She argued politely but angrily, "IT WASN'T EVELINE AND IF YOU KEEP ON SAYING SUCH RUBBISH LIES THEN I'M AFRAID THAT YOU'LL GET A ZERO IN YOUR UPCOMING LANGUAGE EXAMINATION !" roared the ugly witch. Eveline who was behaving in a polite way till now looked at Miss Jones, her eyes had turned red & even her whole face had turned scarlet red. Jim and Sam exchanged horrified looks as they had never seen their bestie like that, though Eveline's face had gone entirely red but still she looked very pretty. Eveline broke the silence and replied furiously "FINE ! If you don't believe me then it's alright but I guess you'll be needed to believe the CCTV cameras, as you had warned them here." She pointed her index finger towards the CCTV camera in the top left corner of the classroom. The entire class looked at the CCTV camera. Miss Jones accepted Eveline's offer but furiously. She yelled at the class, her eyes still at the dark-black haired girl "The class is over ! I, Jim, Sam & Eveline're going to the security office ! When another teacher comes, just tell her that Dorothy ma'am had taken these triplets along with her for some prominent work. Class monitor standup and look over the class !" Alan Matons a stout boy stood up.

When they reached the security office, they had to tell about the whole matter which the ugly witch didn't want to. Clark Watson was there, the security incharge of the orphanage. Eveline asked "Sir could you kindly show us the CCTV footage of last Friday for room number seven, sixth class, section B ?" Clark replied cheerfully "Okay.. wait a minute." He began clicking on the keyboard keys and icons of the computer screen, after a minute or two he spoke up "Time ?" Jim answered before the ugly witch could do so "8:35 in the morning." Clark responded "Fine" , then after a while he spoke up "here it is" Eveline said impatiently "Sir please turn on the audio." Clark did as said. "So now you know how does this reported speech actually work and now I want all of you to revise the rules instantly without any further redo so that I can take your test right now." Miss Jones said in the CCTV footage. "Please forward it a bit." Said Jim , Clark forwarded it to fifty seconds, Jim and Sam had arrived in the CCTV footage by then and were already arguing. "Yes that is it .. Stop right there." Cried out Sam, "Shhh" Miss Jones said to Sam by giving him a furious look. "So boys now I'm afraid to say that if you people will miss another class of mine then I won't just you both, toilets to clean but also you'll be needed to take off your clothes in front of all the classes." Said Miss Jones in the CCTV footage. "See Ma'am, I was right." Said Eveline politely. Miss Jones looked at her angrily and responded "This time you may've saved them but-" "Eve always saves us !" Sam interrupted, the ugly witch looked at her disgustfully and left the security office with a bang of door. "Thank you so much Eve !" Both the boys cried out to Eveline. "If you wouldn't have helped us then that ugly witch would have spared us into p-" "OH SHUT UP !" intruded Eveline in Sam's statement, "I did it just because you people were correct not as I had any sympathy for you two foolish brats !" She yelled with quite rage in her profound voice. Sam asked sadly "Are you still mad on us coz of yesterday ?" Eveline threw a furious look over him and left before they could speak anything else. "Is everything alright with you three ?" Clark asked worriedly, both of them turned to face him, they had entirely forgotten about him that he was also present there listening to there conversation. Sam responded "Ah.. Yeah Sir.. Everything's fine, just a little argument among friends.. You know." Clark smiled at him and replied "Ohk then you can leave now if you don't've any else work." "Yes thank you Sir" Jim thanked him.

They both reached their classroom and didn't dare to look over where Eveline used to sit, when finally Sam looked over to her front seat in the second row, he found out that she was absent. He told Jim about it.. he said hopefully "Perhaps washroom" Sam replied "Yeah I also think that-" "PLUMP PHYSICUE..HOW DARE YOU TALK IN THE CLASS ?" Called out a heavy voice, Sam jumped of fear and turned his head from Jim to where the voice had come from. A blonde-haired boy was standing, a purple-haired girl giggling beside him. "ASON ! YOU HAVE DONE THIS THIRD TIME THIS WEEK !" Sam yelled with frustration and rage in his voice, "Oh, I was doin' timepass .. You know, you two're a nice sort of timepass for me..Right Nadia ?" asked Ason smiling like a dirty toad, "Absolutely" replied Nadia. Sam was about to punch on Ason's face but Jim pulled him back and murmured in his ear "Do you wanna have another lovely meeting with that ugly witch ?" Sam looked at him & then glared at Ason but didn't do anything. At 3, all the students rushed off the class. The two buddies also left and headed straight for the boys' section, when finally they reached; both of them plopped themselves on their respective beds. It was not for the very first time that they had won against Miss Jones because of Eveline but then also they felt contended "I think we should talk to Eve." Sam suggested while breaking up the dead silence, Jim nodded after listening his statement. "But first let us change our clothes." Sam said while getting onto his feet, he began taking off his messy shoes. "Hey talking about robes.. Hmm.. Ah.. Were you actually going to take off your clothes ?" Sam asked curiously, Jim who was removing his smelly socks lifted his head to face him and he was amazed to see Sam curiously happy for the very first time, he responded blankly "Ah.. I dunno" Sam smirked and asked him "Ooo.. Really bro ?" "Yes" Jim replied at once without any delay.

# CHAPTER TWO

# THE ESCAPE

When they had put onto their casual robes they scurried upstairs to the girls' section but were interrupted by Nadia Shimper, "Oo.. What're you boys doing here ?" She asked while giggling. "That's none of your business." Sam replied angrily but Jim grasped his hand & whispered "Control your temper Sam." Sam calmed down and said easily "That has nothing to do with you Nadia." They both were relieved when Nadia was called out by her friend and she went towards her forgetting the two buddies.

When they were going to turn the doorknob- it turned by itself, the wooden oak door swung open and in front of them  a girl with brown eyes, straight jet-black hairs, salmon colored lips; emerged. It was Eveline Guitonnet- a 12 year old girl- The topper and the prettiest girl of the orphanage- Their best friend too. "Oh ! Eve, we were coming to you." Sam said hurriedly, he turned his head towards Jim hoping for him to say something but he didn't, inspite he stood there quietly looking at Eveline's hand which was clutching a card. There was dead silence for next forty seconds, when Eveline turned to go & was about to step forward towards the staircase; Jim blocked her way, Eveline looked at him angrily and said "Let me go !" "I'm extremely sorry Eve." He said while looking at that colorful card in her hand. "I think you should say – We are extremely sorry." Sam told him confusedly while taking a glance of Eveline's eyes. "No.. I'm asking for apologies because I've not wished, I dunno if you've done it or not." Jim explained him, Sam casted a look of confusion over him and asked "What ? I don't understand what you're saying. Why am I supposed to wish Eve ?" Eveline looked at him furiously, Jim said to him "Bro.. Eve's not mad on us because of yesterday." "Then ?" The grey-haired boy asked him, "Today's Eve's birthday and we haven't wished her yet.. Stupid." Jim said at once, Sam asked Eveline quickly "Is today your birthday ?" Eveline stared at him, didn't say anything but her deadly stare answered Sam's unexpected question. Jim pointed his index finger towards the card in Eveline's right hand- HAPPY BIRTHDAY was written on it in bold letters, Sam observed it for a few seconds, he finally looked back at Eveline when Jim stamped his foot on the grey-haired boy's.

"Happy Birthday Eve !" Both of the buddies wished her cheerfully, the girl looked at both of them infuriatedly and turned to go and again as she was about to step forward; Jim blocked her off. "What's wrong with you Eve ?! At least we're wishing, if you won't converse then how will the quarrel be sorted up ?" Sam asked her in one breath. Eveline's face turned to face him. "YOU PEOPLE AREN'T JUST MY CLASSMATES BUT MY BEST FRIENDS SINCE THE AGE OF FIVE. I HAVE ALWAYS WISHED BOTH OF YOU ON YOUR BIRTHDAYS AND NOT JUST THIS, I'VE YOU GIVEN YOU PEOPLE MANY FABULOUS GIFTS TOO. YOU KNOW WHAT, I WAS QUITE A LOT DISTURBED AFTER YESTERDAY'S ARGUMENT BUT STILL WAS EXCITED ABOUT TODAY, I HOPED THAT AT LEAST YOU TWO WILL WISH ME KEEPING OUR

ARGUMENT ASIDE. BUT I WAS TOTALLY WRONG. DO YOU PEOPLE KNOW THAT ALL OF OUR CLASSMATES HAVE WISHED ME ALTHOUGH NEGATIVELY BUT AT LEAST THEY DID SO,EVEN THE SECURITY INCHARGE HAS ALSO .. EVERYBODY HAS WISHED ME EXCEPT FOR MY VERY BEST FRIENDS !" Eveline finished, Sam & Jim were stunned after hearing this speech, they expected it won't end but it ended. Jim said "It's not that I've forgotten your birthday but I wanted to surprise you with a gift & it had taken time." Sam looked at him shockingly- He hadn't seen him engrossed in preparing any gift, so what the hell he's saying ?! Is he lying ? If he is, then Eve would never talk to him. With these thoughts bopping in his head he mumbled in Jim's ear "Are you sure ? I mean I hadn't seen you indulged up. So, from where the hell have you got a gift for her ?!" "From the security office." He responded back to him silently while giving a smile. The one & only thing that added up to his good looks was his lovely smile for sure due to which most of the boys were jealous of him. "What is it ?" Eveline asked uninterestedly though she was quite a lot interested as she knew, if Jim had got a gift for her then it would be ultimately different. "Come with me." Jim replied back. The two followed him.

"This is it." He said while putting a rusty old key in Eveline's soft hands after reaching the boys' section. Eveline gave him a look full of rage and asked urgently "Are you kidding me ? What am I supposed to do of this thing ?!" "Hmm.. Well It's a bit rusty but it's very special for you, actually for not just you but for all of us." Jim replied back joyously. "What d'you mean bro ?" The grey-haired boy asked curiously, "Yes, how is this special for us ?" The girl asked impatiently. "Well.. Remember that day.. Eve, when you said that you don't wanna live here anymore."

Jim said questioningly. Eveline nodded. "Hmm..you wished that were you had the main gate's keys so that you can escape from this hell. So I thought to give you liberty as a birthday gift, I thought to leave this hell and therefore I had stolen this key from the security office." Jim said profoundly. Eveline was listening him with rapt attention but when he finished saying, her eyes were full of tears not of rage but of merriment as Jim took quite big risk for her birthday gift. What if he had got caught ? What if someone had seen him ? She had never ever imagined that she could really escape from that ruddy hell but now only because of her best buddy finally the time has come of their departure. She moved closer to him and hugged him tightly and said "Thank you so much Jim !" Sam back hugged the two and said "Finally we can leave this hell, and just because of you. .BRO !" They all laughed, their eyes bulged with tears of happiness. They all looked contended as after a very long period of time finally they would be escaping the hell, their prolonged wish had come true. The triplets decided to escape in the night as it would be the most suitable time to do so because the entire orphanage would be asleep by that time.

By 1'o clock there wasn't any voice, if there was then only the voice of the clock which had struck one. Jim got to his feet quietly, put on his shoes and moved towards Sam's bed where he found him to be laying awake already, it seemed like he was waiting for him to come. Sam got up from his bed, put on his shoes and they both picked up their bags full of apparels, toothbrushes, food, piggy banks and other important stuff. Quietly they tiptoed up to the door from between the loud snores of the children and more quietly they closed the door. When they turned to go upstairs they saw they wouldn't need to do so, as

Eveline was standing there, a few inches away with her large bag of which the two buddies were, a hundred and one percent sure was to be full of books. "How many books have you filled in it ?" Sam asked her by giving a nasty look to the bag, "Books ? Sam, why am I supposed to take books along with me ?" She asked sharply while they were going downstairs. "So, aren't you carrying any books in it ?" He asked urgently with a shock in his voice. "Obviously not.. What am I supposed to do of those books ? I have read them all." Eveline said swiftly, "Can't you two keep quiet ?!" Jim said at once, he continued "If anyone caught us then we'll be hanged for sure." "Okay, we'll be quiet now." They both responded together. When finally they reached the ground floor, it was quite a lot dark for them to watch out, even they were unable to see each other. Jim took out a flashlight from the side pocket of his bag and switched it on. "It's better." Jim said to himself. It was the main hall, they tiptoed up to the main door. "Where is the key ?" Jim asked quickly while checking his pockets. "It's here." Eveline responded while handing him the key, "You've forgotten to take it back." She explained, Jim took the key and silently began to unlock the lock. Sam & Eveline exchanged merry looks, they couldn't believe their eyes as they had never imagined that- one day they would be free to do anything; one day they would actually escape the orphanage, and this all is about to happen just because of a dark-blue haired, azure colored eyes, fit and sturdy boy – Jim Sueruds. "It's not getting unlocked." Jim said looking terrified. "What ?! Wait.. Give me, let me try." Sam said while taking the key and began putting efforts." "Sam ! You're doing it incorrectly, you're needed to turn it right not left. Wait, hand it to me." Eveline said annoyingly, Jim who thought – I was also doing it in the same way, kept quiet. Suddenly they heard a crack voice from the lock, they moved closer to see what had happened. It had unlocked, "It has unlocked !" Sam cried. "Shhh" The other two instructed angrily, Jim removed the lock from the door and put it in his bag. "What will you do with it ?" Sam asked curiously, "Nothing" He replied back to him simply. Jim pushed the door and it swung open, after a prolonged period of time they had seen the beautiful sky full of stars. "Let's go." Jim said to the other two cheerfully. The three of them set onto their feet and walked a few steps then turned to get a last glance of the place where they had spent eight pain-staking years of their life together then they turned and left.

"What's the time ?" Sam asked while giving an exhausted look to the two. "Half past two." Jim replied back, "We've been walking from an hour !" Sam said exhaustedly, "Well, I suppose we've come quite far away from the orphanage, it is midnight and now we've entered the forest area too.. and I suppose all of us would be exhausted after constantly strolling for a whole hour.. So I think let us stay here for this night. What do you two think of that ?" Jim asked swiftly, "YUP ! I'm very tired." "Yes.. You're right Jim." Sam and Eveline said together respectively in one go. The three were in the woods, standing under the shade of a big old banyan tree, they sat down there, putting their bags together behind them. Eveline looked at Jim and said "Jim.. I did not have a single thought that your gift for my birthday would be liberty for us, but this is the best gift ever, but don't you think that you took quite big risk for it ?" Jim turned his face from the sky towards her face which was shining due to the moonlight falling on her face, he looked at her for a while, then said to her "Well, yeah it was a risk but not as much big as our freedom is and I don't worth it more than my best buddies." Eveline smiled at him while Sam said to him "Bro.. You're our best friend ! Okay.. Guys, I think we should take an oath right now that we won't ever segregate from one another and will always be there for each other in future, in happiest as well as the grimmest times like we've been till now." Jim and Eveline looked at him and responded cheerfully "Of course !" The tree buddies swore to god, "Okay now listen to my jokes, I've got many and I've waited a lot to tell them to you guys." Sam said impatiently, "Yup.. Go ahead." The two replied cheerfully, "Tell me.. What do bees use to fix their hair ?" Sam asked impatiently but merrily, "How would I know ?" Eveline answered without any redo. Sam asked Jim "What d'you think about it ? Any guesses ?" Jim answered swiftly at once "Na.. Bro, dunno." "Oh dumbs ! HONEYCOMBS !" Sam replied and laughed heartily, the else two kept quiet for a while, looked at one another then they pretended to laugh too. "OK.. Now tell me, how many fingers do we have ?" Sam asked as he saw the other two laughing. "OH ! I know that, we've 8 fingers in total." Eveline responded impatiently, "Stupid.. We have 24 fingers in total." Sam corrected her "How ?!" She asked quickly, "Eve, we're three here and I guess Sam included our fingers too in his own. Am I right dude ?" Jim asked him smartly "Absolutely" He responded back cheerfully and began to laugh, Jim also giggled while Eveline looked at both of them ridiculously, "Ok now tell me-" "Stop now.. I'm feeling dizzy.. I'm sleeping. Goodnight" Eveline intruded in Sam's statement and she laid down while getting the support of the tree's massive roots, she put her bag as a pillow at the back of her head and closed her eyes. "Night" The two buddies replied back to her.

"By the way.. Bro, d'you remember the ugly witch's words to Eve about us ?" Sam asked the blue-haired boy who was looking into the sky, after sometime after confirming that Eveline was fast asleep , "Which words ?" He asked without looking at him "She referred us as her 'boyfriends'." Sam told him impatiently "Hmm.. So what ?" Jim asked him back blankly "So.. What d'you think about it ?" The grey-haired boy asked him back "About what ?" Jim asked him while turning his head from the sky to him. "Hmm.. I mean what do you think that why the ugly witch considered us to be her 'boyfriends' ?" He asked urgently "Well.. I think that's coz Eve spends most of her time with us and also that ugly witch wanted to disrespect Eveline constantly after what her sister did to his son. So I guess that might've been one most prominent reason for her to do so." Jim answered him after thinking for a minute. "But there wasn't any of our Eve's fault in it, it has nothing to do with her. So why ? You know what bro, sometimes I felt like I should've killed her, she knew it very well that it was not Eve's fault at all but still she kept disrespecting her by calling her 'profitable bookworm'." Sam said furiously "Well.. I also felt the same like what you did but we couldn't do so and we shouldn't have either did it as it would be incorrect." Jim said while putting his hand on his bro's shoulder, "Hmm.. Yeah you're right. But I'm quite happy for that we're no longer there, now no one can tease us, beat us or torture us ! OH BRO ! I'm really very happy ! After spending eight grimmest years of our life in there finally we've been set off free only coz of you.. BRO ! Thank you ! Oh dude I love you so much as a buddy !" Sam said happily and hugged Jim, Jim patted at the back of his head and replied "You consider me as your best friend and now you're thanking me.. Dude there's no 'thank you' and 'sorry' in best buddies, remember." Jim said happily, "After my parents' demise I never ever considered anyone as my family as no one ever cared for me, but, only you thought so, after getting you in my life it changed entirely.. I didn't know how to tie up shoelaces as I lost my parents at a very small age.. I was nonplussed when I saw physics' derivations but you changed this novice into a master. I-" "Oh, stop bro" Jim interrupted coolly in Sam's unending sentimental speech. "We're buddies and buddies never thank each other for their deeds for one another." Jim said happily.

# CHAPTER THREE

# THE STRANGE PORTAL

The next morning Eveline was the first to wake up, she looked at her old watch which her uncle had gifted her at the age of four, it was half past seven, she turned to look at her friends – they were still asleep & Sam's snores were so loud that she was needed to thrust her fingers in her ears.. She casted a disgustful look over him. She got up and thought to look for a water resource so that she can get herself off from the dust and dirt before Sam & Jim could wakeup. She opened her bag and took out a towel, some neat robes, a toothbrush etc. But the trouble was how would she recognize the path back to the boys, at the moment she got an idea; She unzipped Sam's bag and took out a piece of chalk – She was quite sure that she would definitely find a piece of chalk as Sam had an ultimate love of drawing sketches out of pieces of chalk- It was his first love and that is why he was so good in art than the two; In fact, Eveline & Jim were nothing in front of Sam ( A young artist) - he could copy any picture so good that they looked facsimile. She began ambling keeping in mind to make a X on the trees coming in her way, after sometime she heard the sound of water falling from an ample amount of height, she ran in that direction while drawing crosses on trees by which she was passing by and after sometime; She found a big waterfall. With a delightful and scrutinizing look in all four directions, she took off her apparels and jumped up into the crystal clear water, the water was cold but Eveline did like the natural shower, she loved it. She got off from the water after sometime, quickly wrapped a towel around herself and wore her robes after drying her body. Then she brushed up her teeth and hairs. When she was done of all the chores, she started to stroll back up to her buddies. The moment she made it to that place, she found her friends looking pretty scared and were conversing to one another, while she hid behind a bush.

"Now where will we find her ?" Sam asked horribly while Jim replied back "She should've told us or should've left a note.. She's so fool !" "Yes ! She's a fool !" Sam agreed to his bro's statement, "Hey, I'm here. Stop calling me 'fool'." Came out a voice from behind a bush that was just next to Jim and out emerged a girly figure of Eveline. They swiveled & were delighted to see their studious friend though they were still furious on her for being a careless girl, Jim spilled his anger on her by yelling "WHERE WERE YOU ?! HOW CAN YOU BE CARELESS THAT YOU RAN OFF WITHOUT TELLING ANYONE OF US ?! AT LEAST, YOU SHOULD HAVE MADE US AWARE BY LEAVING A NOTE IF YOU WERE HAVIN' TROUBLE BY AROUSING !" Eveline got scared a bit after hearing these yells of her caring friend but she mustered courage to respond back "I thought I would be back in a while before you people would arouse. Ah.. I had gone to search for a water resource so that I can get a bath and freshen up." "Whatever ! But you should've told us, Eve !" Sam said to her angrily, Eveline looked at both of them and apologized "I'm sorry, I do accept, it was my fault that I didn't tell anybody of you. I'm extremely sorry." The boys looked at her, she looked at them with tears of regret. "Hmm.. Fine, we're forgiving you this time just coz it's your first mistake but we won't, next time." Sam responded back to her while looking at his bro who looked terrified giving death stares to Eveline though she didn't notice that. "Ah.. I think, you people should also bathe and get yourself off this mud and dirt as not so far is a big waterfall and Do not worry of the pathway, I've made crosses on trees. Just follow them." Eveline said to them swiftly, "Hmm..That's pretty great, okay; Bro you can go first." Sam responded, Jim answered "Fine" and he took off similar things like Eveline did and left. After sometime he returned and Sam went.

Jim looked at Eveline who was having her hotdog; After a while he moved towards her and said "I'm sorry.. Eve. I had yelled on you so rudely." After saying these words he moved back to his place, Eveline looked at him, smiled and replied back "I'm not mad on you and I shouldn't be, it was my fault at all. It's all fine for a friend to yell on his friend ; It's a way of showing affection towards your friend and we're not just friends but best friends." Jim gave her his most appealing smile and said "I'm happy that you're not furious but I'm also hungry. Won't you share your hotdog like you always did ?" Eveline laughed and handed him half of her hotdog while he also gave half of his pancake. They both had just begun to enjoy their breakfast suddenly Sam emerged out of nowhere and said loudly "How can you people be so mean ? Can't you wait ?" "Bro.. There's quite left for you." Jim replied to him while handing a sandwich and a hotdog. Sam took them urgently and began gobbling up to which Eveline passed a look of disgust and advised him to eat slowly to which she got nothing else than ignorance.

It was 8:45, all of them were sitting there thinking critically about what would they do now ? Would they ever be able to fulfill their respective dreams ? Would their dreams ever come true ? Had they done wrong by escaping off the orphanage where they were getting education although in pains ? The triplets minds' were full with these thoughts, they looked extremely worried about their future. Suddenly Sam asked worriedly "Guys, d'you think I possess the potential of becoming a great artist ?" Eveline replied back "Yes Sam, there's no doubt about it." "Absolutely, I do not doubt your talent." Jim agreed "But why do you ask so ?" He asked him, to which his bro bombarded questions like "What are we supposed to do now ? D'you people have any idea about what we'll do in future ? Will we ever be able to fulfill our dreams ? Will you be able to become a scientist, Jim ? Will you become a successful person, Eve ? WILL WE EVER BE ABLE TO BECOME WHAT WE WANNA ? WILL-" "Oh stop, bro; Stop, put a full stop to your questions." Jim intruded to the unending list of questions asked by Sam. After thinking for while Jim said "I think we should do something.. I mean we're needed to get a job as soon as possible so that we can complete our education and then only our dreams would come true. I hope you people can get me, cause no pain no gain." "Yes.. You're absolutely right, Jim. We need to get some work; I think we should get up from here and try to find a way out of these woods. What do you guys say ?" Eveline asked swiftly "Yes, let's get onto our feet and find a way out of this jungle." The boys agreed and said together.

It was 21$^{st}$ of April, summer had just begun but still the sun's rays felt like hot burning fireballs, the trees they were facing now were quite lean in comparison to the trees the three had seen before, there were many trees which were laden with colorful & tempting fruits but the triplets had no idea of swallowing them as they were quite aware of the fact that not all the fruits are edible, many of them could be venomous and it won't be a good idea to ingest anything without knowing about it accurately and precisely. At this time, many of the plantings by which they were passing by were entirely dried up which showed the triumph of the sun over the greenery.

"Oh my goodness ! Can anyone pick me up ? My energy's completely drained off." Sam said exhaustedly while looking at his friends hopefully, "No one's gonna pick you up . If you had expected us to carry you on our backs or in our bags then it's not so and it won't be so as well." Eveline replied nastily at once.

"If you can't help then at least don't taunt me, stay quiet." Sam said rapidly while glaring at her, "Who the hell are you to tell me to stay silent ?! I will not stay silent. I'll keep talking." Eveline said with a bit of rage in her profound voice, "Oh ! I don't talk to rude girls." Sam said bitterly, to this savage statement he was about to get a response from the smart girl but the blue-haired boy spoke up "Stop it you two ! I won't bear any single word of yours ! Can't you two stroll forth keeping your mouths shut for one another ?!" "He was the first to speak rudely, he should've-" "I dunno who spoke first and I don't wanna know either ! You two, just do me favour, keep your mouths shut until and unless we've found a suitable job & place to live, for us." Jim intruded in the girl's statement.

The triplets kept ambling until Jim had his eyes on his wristwatch which had struck 12, they had been walking for 3 hours, they stopped their steps when Jim made them aware of the time.

"Let's get down here for sometime and have rest." Jim said, the two did as told and that's when their water bottles turned out to be empty, Jim decided to look for a water resource & get some water as they would definitely need it for their upcoming journey, therefore he got to his dusty feet with a chalk piece in one hand and their water bottles in another hand and left.

"What d'you think about which job you'll get ?" Sam asked after a while, to which the dark black-haired girl responded "Hmm.. I don't know but I'll make sure that the job which I'll be doing can't consume more time of mine so that I can utilize that time in my studies." "What bout you ? Which job you want to do ?" She asked, Sam thought for a while then replied after a minute or two "Hmm.. I wanna do a job that can actually help me out in my future, I mean something like painting or sketching." "Oh, that's nice. This would absolutely help you in your career." Eveline said smiling widely.

On the other hand, Jim had found a stream with sweet but clean water which he had filled in his water bottles after doing that he should've left but he didn't do it instead he found himself indulged in spotting something weirdly shining that was behind a bush, he moved towards it daringly and saw a very giant gate-like structure. It was though looking like a gate but was not. Without thinking for a while the blue-haired boy began to run back by following the trees with cross marks up to his friends, at last when he reached & told them, they didn't believe him until they witnessed the weird gate by their self eyes.

"What d'you think this is ?" Sam asked while looking at the gate-like thing incredulously, "It's a portal." Eveline replied swiftly without looking at him as she was observing the portal precisely along with Jim. "What's that ?" The grey-haired boy asked curiously "A portal's a gateway between two or more dimensions or a teleportation device, it works as an entrance via which an individual can actually visit any other dimension across the universe or it can teleport individuals." Jim responded while observing the portal attentively. Sam looked at him for a second then said incredibly "Does that mean we can go to another world through this portal ?" "Yes" Eveline replied turning her head from the portal to Sam while Jim kept looking at it carefully. "That's-That's amazing." The young artist cried enthusiastically. He had never imagined if he could actually visit another world along with his best buddies, he was about to jump into the portal but felt to be pulled back by his shirt's collar and the one to pull him back was none other than Eveline. "What ? What's the reason behind pulling me like this ?" Sam asked rapidly, to which Eveline replied "Coz.. I don't consider this act to be safe. Do you also think that, Jim ?" "Well, I don't think that, Eve, cause we're already stuck in a dense forest and do you consider this jungle to be secure for us ?" Jim answered after thinking for a while, "You're saying right but is it all fine to go to another dimension ? I mean to say if we couldn't survive there." The girl said swiftly "Eve.. We'll get it only when we'll dare to go." Sam replied quickly. "Ah.. Fine, I agree to come." Eveline said hesitantly. "Okay ! Everyone hold one another's hands and we will jump on, my count of three." Jim said energetically, they seized each other's hands and stood straight with a bit of fear in their eyes as they didn't know what was waiting for them in that dimension. "Okay.. One, two and.. Three." Jim said pronouncing every word carefully and they pranced. The triplets' eyes were shut, they only got opened when they had made sure that nothing dangerous was around by waiting for sometime. And when they finally opened them, they felt quite dizzy, Sam was about to fell but Jim & Eveline grabbed him tightly.

They looked around to notice nothing else than a gigantic pool of boiling lava. There wasn't a single planting over there, only dried up reddish soil along with some dried twigs. The sky was orange in color. The geographical conditions wholly indicate that neither human beings nor flora-fauna can adapt there, Eveline was going to ask the two boys if they could survive there when Sam spoke up "What the hell is this place ! Too hot ! This is even worse than the sun in our dimension." "I'm sorry, Eve. I can't tolerate this hotness anymore, let-let's get back to our world." Sam continued rapidly as Eveline was about to speak up. Then she spoke "I had told you people before, but you two had the curiosity. Anyways, let's go-" "Oh my goodness ! New students !" Interrupted a high-pitched voice from their behind.

They swiveled to see an old lady coming towards them who was dressed in a dark green gown, wrapped in a red shawl with golden stripes on it and her gray hairs pinned back in a big bundle that looked like a bun with a pretty bow on top. She had wrinkles on her whole face but her way of walking said the converse of her looks, it showed her sturdiness and fitness. Though she was old but still looked very beautiful. "Who's this ?" Sam asked whisperingly while staring at her, "How would we know, Sam ? We're also standing here with you, noticing her for the very first time." Eveline mumbled back to him. "And Don't mumble otherwise she would hear you." She continued slowly, to which Sam said fiercely "Stop advising me, I'm not a child anymore." Sam whispered bitterly, "I'm not advising you, just telling." Eveline murmured at once,

Sam was going to give a convincing argument to that statement of hers when Jim burst out of anger and whispered alarmingly "Guys, stop it ! Look into the delicacy of time. Kindly keep your argument aside for sometime." "Ok.. I won't say anything now but I'll surely-" "Sam !" Jim whispered with vexation. "Fine" He mumbled at once.

Although the lady's way of stepping forward seemed to be sturdy but her speed was a bit slow which took her too long to make it to the children.

# CHAPTER FOUR

# MILANTONS MYTHICAL WORLD

"Good Afternoon.. Actually we've come from this portal-" "Oh I know that.. My dear !" The old lady interrupted when Eveline began to explain, she smiled widely looking at the three children to which Sam looked at her with disgust while Eveline smiled back and Jim gave no reaction. "You know what, it's so warm in here, I don't suppose you live here or do you ?" Sam asked still giving her a disgustful look, "Of course, I don't, I live in MMW." The lady responded still smiling wildly "MMW ?" The triplets said in a questioning manner along with confused looks, to which the lady replied "Milantons Mythical World" "That sounds interesting but what's it ?" Jim asked curiously "Oh well; It needs a brief explanation as there's lot to be told bout it and it deserves too but I can tell in short. So, MMW is a magical world where everything's magical from mouth-watering delicious dishes to fancy stylish clothes, from fantastic mythical monuments to incredible weird fauna, from foremost tourist spots to amazing fantasy stories." finished the old lady nostalgically.

The three children were dumbstruck as they can't believe on what they've heard; But it was really true. "M-

Magic ?! I don't think any such thing like that exists in this universe, science is all what I know and it has been proven that magic is just an amazing feat of hands." Jim spoke up confidently, "Hmm.. Seems like you love science but unfortunately it's not like what you said, magic do exist. Yes it is in real." Said the old lady politely while smiling at him. "I don't believe you & wouldn't do so either until and unless I've got something as a proof." Said Jim seriously but politely, "What's there to prove in that ? It is true." Said the lady still smiling at him, "Why do you expect us to believe on your false statements ? You keep on saying that a hundred or a thousand times but I'm not going to take your saying as true." Jim said seriously, again while keeping in mind to be polite. "Smart boy; Not a single person has ever asked this to me in my entire duration of life till now, everyone has given shocking reactions but none of them has ever reacted like you boy, your name ?" Said the old lady impressively, "Jim Sueruds" Jim said at once, "Those persons would've admitted your words recklessly, that is why they didn't question you but our buddy Jim ain't like those." Sam said profoundly while patting proudly at Jim's shoulder. "Hmm.. Well, you want proof, right ?" The lady asked while smiling at the three, "Yes" Said the triplets together in same voice. "All well, let me prove it to you." The old lady said confidently still smiling wildly.

The old lady stood silently for a second then she began to swivel her hands constantly, after which she began her hands to move like making a sphere. The three children were not flickering their eyes for even a second specially the blue-haired boy, after a while a yellowish ball out of which hot flames were emerging was ready in the old lady's palms; To this sight the triplets gave an astonished reaction which was simply obvious too. After sometime the old lady allowed the fireball to vanish out from there by saying "Vanisho !" which was indeed another magical trick for the innocent 12 year olds who hadn't sighted anything like this before though imagined in dreams. The three stared open-mouthed in surprise, Sam said "Bro pinch me, I can't trust on what I've seen right now." Eveline pinched him instead of his bro after noticing Jim being dumbstruck responding nothing. The old lady laughed and said "Now, I think there's nothing left not to trust on indiscriminately. Right or not ?" "Absolutely not, now we-we do trust you." Eveline said impatiently after waiting for his blue-haired buddy to reply. Sam hit Jim by his elbow gently, allowing him to get back to his senses, "Ah.. I take my words back but I still can't believe, I mean I do admit that what I witnessed is absolutely not fake but it's incredulous." Said Jim at once after realizing his earlier words to the old lady, "I know, it's indeed unbelievable and seriously incredible too but it is true." The old lady said while patting at the back of the triplets.

"So, where's that MMW, miss-ah ?" "Masarah" Responded the lady to Sam, "Oh, Is that your sur-" "You can simply call me Masarah" Interrupted the lady hesitantly into Sam's statement. "Oh, but you're-" "Do as I say." The old lady said at once while intruding in Eveline's sentence, only Jim got a glance of her tensed face which wasn't so a second ago, Jim wondered why it had turned so. "All well, now introduce yourselves as well." Said the lady rapidly, "Hello, I am Eveline Guitonnet. Nice to meet you, Masarah !" "Hello I'm Sam Mahongthan. Pleased to meet you." "Hi Masarah, well you know my name. Glad to meet you." Said the three one after another; "I'm also pleased to meet you three." Masarah said smiling widely, "Well, so where's that MMW ?" Jim & Sam asked in one voice, "Oh ! It's there."

Replied Masarah while pointing her index finger towards the ocean overflowing with lava. The children looked where her finger pointed and they were certainly shocked after realizing the location, Sam asked ridiculously "What d'you mean by that ? Are you sayin' that MMW exists there ? But is it actually possible ?" "Everything's possible if we possess magic." Said Masarah with her eyes shining brightly along with an obvious confidence "Hmm.. How d'you get there ?" Sam asked without any reaction, "Well.. I don't get there all by myself instead I take somebody's help." Masarah responded after clearing her throat "Whose help ? I am unable to view anyone except for the four of us." Asked Eveline confusedly while looking around expecting to spot someone else than them "Looks like it's time for my pet's introduction." Masarah responded after which she called out heavily in a loud voice " SUPIE ! Come out baby ! It's time for you to make new friends." The triplets looked around but saw nobody and they wondered to whom Masarah was referring to by saying 'Supie' if there was not a single body across them. Sam thought if they had got themselves introduced to a mad old lady suddenly the terra firma set about onto an unanticipated abrupt drop down motion due to which the triplets didn't just exchange horrified looks with each other but they tumbled due to sudden motion made by the dusty dry land; "What the hell is happening ! What have you done ?! Wanna ki-" Sam was unable to complete his sentence when Jim elbowed him to look at what they were looking with terrified expressions.

The lava was splattering hither & tither bones out came a peculiar creature at which they looked along with incredible faces, it was certainly unbelievable to them as out came up a very giant dark green-colored scaly creature having big sturdy and unusual bat-wings and also a big tail which was approximately five hundred meters long, also the creature had spikes on the top of his back, somewhat the creature looked like dracorex to Eveline – a pachycephalosaur from the end of cretaceous period which used to live in USA 66 million years ago. The creature turned out to be a giant dragon when it stood in front of the triplets at a distance of fifty-five meters; They weren't frightened to see a dragon for the first time in their lives but were not amused as well. "Good boy.. You waited until I called out to you; I'll certainly give you a reward for your good deed. Anyways, meet your newest friends." Said Masarah amusedly while pointing her hand towards Jim, Sam & Eveline after which she patted at the dragon's toenail, the beast drew his sizeable yellowish eyes at them & moved closer to the jet black haired girl and licked her leaving her wrenched thoroughly but Eveline patted at his head with her shivering hands; Sam gave the creature a nasty look and took a few steps backwards to avoid himself to be in the indifferent state like his friend was. But unfortunately the dragon noticed him backing away & he took just a half-meter step to turn the boy into the same state as well. And then came Jim's turn who didn't back away but the dragon didn't lick him in spite of doing that, the beast grasped him in his mouth & threw him to land on his head, for a moment Jim expected his death to be near but when he got himself seated on the dragon's top of head he felt relieved; He didn't understand why the dragon manifested more affection for him than his own master, he only got it when he got hold of his right wing on which Jim perceived a brown scar, Jim realized something and shouted out to his friends with joy "Sam ! Eveline ! This is our Ro !" "What ? How can it be possible ? This is a dragon Jim, not our Ro !" Eveline shouted out to him (as Jim was sitting at the top of dragon's head) "Yes.. I know but I'm hundred and one percent sure it's it !" Jim shouted back to her joyfully while Sam said to Eveline "Has he gone crazy or what ? How can a bat turn out to be a dragon ?" "It can" Masarah responded back to him profoundly "Eh ?" Sounded the two, "Yup, a bat can turn out to be a dragon." She said to them "But how ?" Asked the two together "Magic, anything's possible becoz of magic." Replied Masarah confidently while smiling widely. "Oh really, I don't think it would be possible to sneeze with eyes opened up." Murmured Sam, to which Masarah responded "Yes it is possible." Sam looked at her astonishingly but said nothing.

When the dark blue-haired boy got off the giant beast he looked very pleased and excited after seeing his Ro after a prolonged period of time, Ro was his pet bat which he had saved from the hold of Ason & his boys' gang who intended to asphyxiate him by throwing him into the nearby pool of the orphanage, he did it at the age of eight from that time he had this bat with him and he christened it 'Ro', but after a few years, one day Jim couldn't find Ro into the orphanage he searched for him even interrogated to each student studying out there but unluckily was unable to find his pet bat, Jim blamed himself for not taking care of Ro due to which he flew away, he wept a lot for his misdeed; But was heated up when he got to know that Ason along with his boys' gang and Miss Jones had thrown his pet bat out of the orphanage. After that Jim & his two buddies never ever got to see their pet bat Ro back.

"So did you transformed Ro into a dragon ?" Eveline asked with utter curiosity "Yes, cause I was being told to get a means by which students can travel." Masarah replied back to her, the triplets looked confused, one of them with grey hairs asked "Students ? Do you have students in your

MMW ? Are you a teacher ?" "No I'm certainly not but there're indeed students in MMW studying in OMSOM." Masarah responded profoundly to which Sam questioned again "What d'you mean by OMSOM ?" "Oh, by OMSOM I meant Olaskovocik Mantonious School Of Magic- The only magical school in MMW." Masarah responded while wiping the sweat in between her lips and a nose with many black hades at the tip "Woah ! Such a big name !" Cried out Eveline with joy on her face, "Yes but it doesn't only possess a big name, It does possess ample reputation as well." Masarah responded nonchalantly and confidently.

"These all things sound amazing, the students who study in OMSOM get to know about magic, I guess." Said Eveline excitedly "They do not study bout magic they study magic." Replied Masarah back to her immediately as she heard her. "Hmm.. I wish I could also get an opportunity to study there." Sam said to his two buddies, "Of course you can." Replied Masarah cheerfully in a casual way "Really ?" Sam asked in return to her astonishing statement which wasn't so to her but it was so for the children "Yes absolutely you can." She said at once profoundly while grinning like a Cheshire cat, this grin of hers wasn't repellent to Sam this time like most of the times it was so. He beamed back to her and had thought of praising her for making such a statement but leaved that thought of him after he got a glimpse of Eveline's face which seemed to ask him mutely 'What about our financial condition ?'

"Ah.. Masarah our financial condition is not so." Eveline said to her sadly while looking at Sam's disappointed face while Jim didn't had a bit of sorrow on his handsome face like he was saying – It's the truth we can't deny to admit it and he said to Masarah beamingly when she asked them about their parents "We have no parents." Sam got startled after sighting Jim's grinning face while telling that, as he had never did that ago whereas Eveline thought it to be appalling for her as she considered that, her friend is changing quite rapidly as he was the boy who always had shiny pearls in his eyes for his parents' demise and when anybody asked him about his guardians he had no reply for it, he always remained mute for such an asking but this was for the very first time that he had responded back & that too with a grin. Jim looked back at his friends and beamed at them too; His eyes said clearly 'We can't do anything about it and our parents never taught us to weep, they always taught us to stay sturdy in front of others although we can weep in front of our closer ones but to shed tears in front of strangers would manifest our weakness, it'd make us look feeble.' Eveline smiled back to him while Sam manifested a thumbs up to him.

"Well, I'm damn sure our great headmaster and headmistress won't deny you people from learning even if you don't possess finances if you really have a wanting for it." Masarah said sympathetically while taking a glance of Supie who was constantly observing his not so old master – Jim, "By the way, do you children have your own bank accounts ?" Asked Masarah rapidly "Yes but we don't know where's the bank, our parents didn't tell us bout it." Replied Eveline at once "Oh do not worry for that, I'll let your bank accounts to shift from that bank to our MMW's, one & only bank." Continued she happily "Bank ? Which bank ?" "You'll get to know after sometime." Masarah answered Sam.

"Okay Jim, Sam & Eveline, I'll be needed to head off to pick up students from different dimensions... Oh I forgot to tell you; That's my job." Masarah said while looking at the three's confused faces. "So, we should immediately leave for MMW. Just do as I say." Masarah responded commandingly, to which the three of them nodded obediently, in return Masarah smiled back to them like a toad which was actually very repellent for Sam this time but he resisted his thought of replying back to her to stop beaming constantly for no reason. He did this just because Masarah had actually turned out to be angel for the three of them who would actually change their lives from a hell to heaven and he should be grateful for that, he shouldn't react like he's stone-hearted.

Masarah ordered Supie to sit down but he didn't do it, Supie was expecting his actual master to command him the same, his eyes seemed to say that; Jim understood it at the moment Supie looked at him but he didn't order him instead he patted at his head and said sweetly "Ro, kindly obey your mistress's order." "No Jim I'm not his mistress. You are his master; I used to wonder why he remained so quiet & sad, he never enjoyed the most expensive finger-licking dishes like other dragons did, I thought he's distinguished but the actual reason was that he was missing his actual owner. But now I won't let him to get departed from you, I can't do such a sin, if I'd known the reality then I swear I'd not have done it as neither I had any intention nor any-" "It's all fine, Masarah, in fact I don't think you did anything wrong, in the orphanage we used to live, was a hell for not just the three of us but for Ro too, & I'd not want Ro to live with me in that hell either, it was my destiny that I found him and it was his luck that he found you." Jim intruded in Masarah's emotional explanation (as while explaining large droplets were trickling down her wrinkled cheeks) "Yeah Masarah Jim's right; By the way we were talking bout leaving." Said Sam reminding her of that enthusiastic thought (for him) "Oh yeah, I'd be late. Ok now Supie kindly sit down." Said Masarah while wiping her moist cheeks.

Supie sat down only for the sake of his master's request to obey Masarah's order although he didn't intended to do so. As he sat down, Masarah along with Eveline & Sam had struggled a bit to climb up to his back while Jim wasn't needed to use his own strength as again the beast had clutched him softly in his sizeable mouth keeping in mind not to hurt his master and had thrown securely onto the top of his head; Where Jim was sitting onto the top of Supie's head, the others were sitting on the dragon's back. This manifested the dragon's obedience, gratitude, selfless love & esteem just for Jim, though Sam & Eveline were also Ro's all time favorite partners but the place Jim had in the dragon's mind and heart couldn't be replaced by anybody else not even by his own mum.

"Ok.. now, stay quiet for a moment." "Survivio !" Masarah said pronouncing the spell precisely and that was when she pointed her hands on the children one after another & out came a big pure white ray of light from her wrinkled hands, divided into five tiny rays and set about to enter into the five individuals via their chests.

"Ok now Supie you know what to do." Said Masarah smiling widely while caressing his back.

At the moment the dragon heard those words he flapped his giant sturdy wings and set about onto a flight, at first not at much speed & height but later he gained speed along with height.

"Tell us more about OMSOM." Said Eveline politely "Oh I knew you'd ask me that, as I had smelled a studious feeling from you." Masarah said while smiling "Smelled ?" "Well, I do possess a caliber of getting smells of individuals and then getting their capability, in easy words I have an ability of getting others' ability. Like for example I get the smell of an outstanding artist from you, Sam." Masarah explained to Sam. "Oh ! That's excellent. Well, actually Eveline used to be a continuous topper of our orphanage's school, she's fond of books and such stuff." Sam said in a heralding tone while taking a glimpse of Eveline going red, "That's pretty amazing, looks like Tulip's about to get a tough competitor quite soon." Masarah said beamingly "Tulip ? Who's that ?" Asked Sam after Eveline had ended saying "That'll be great, I'll love competing with her." "Well, like Eveline's a topper; Tulip Albatross is also a constant topper of OMSOM from past six years." Masarah said profoundly, Sam lifted up his eyebrows and asked unbelievably "What ! Six long years ! I dunno how these toppers maintain their lead."

The dragon began to fly down and after sometime he dived into the boiling hot lava, at this act of him, the triplets shrieked but when they realized that they were actually under lava & their bodies were all well, not a single burn was on them, they were relieved and when Sam asked Masarah about it, she told him that she had casted a spell on them earlier.

After about half an hour they viewed a big board with three words written in bold – 'THE GREAT TUNNELS', the time was half past two. "Finally ! Now, Supie you know very well what's next." Masarah said delightedly, to which Supie nodded his head so hard that Jim tripped over from the top of it but how could his Ro let anything happen to him if he was there ? Supie dived down and caught him on his head's top then the giant beast turned right & gilded into a tunnel with a side board with '464' written on it in bold. The tunnel just seemed dark from outside but was nicely lit by fire torches when Sam asked the reason behind lava not able to enter the tunnel, he was answered by Masarah that they seriously would not want lava in their world.

Suddenly there was large bright flash which had caused them to shut their eyes except for Supie, when finally they allowed their eyelids to open, they were amused to see that they had made it to Milantons Mythical World as they sighted a giant board – 'WELCOME TO MILANTONS MYTHICAL WORLD'.

The giant peculiar beast terminated his flight as their journey had come to a cease, he stopped with a jerk that everybody tumbled off from his back exempting Jim, it wasn't Ro who was able to prevent him from falling but it was Jim himself to let him not to tumble off as he had landed on his two feet securely just because of his hobby of learning newest feats along with his dad earlier & later in the orphanage all by himself lonely at nights, due to which he had come to a perfection and had turned out to be a stunt-person just for himself.

"Oh.. I am really sorry, It's his faux pas to terminate every flight with a jerk." Said Masarah with ingenuity, while rubbing her waist she continued saying as Jim helped her to get up "It's incorrigible." "Oh my ankle ! This beast !" Sam yelled bitterly at Supie who was now caressing his sturdy wings, while Eveline murmured to herself which Jim heard "This beast is a disaster ! But how Jim landed so safely ?!" After hearing this comment plus question of his girl-friend he giggled and gave her a hand allowing her to get back onto her feet, after which he helped Sam to stand up to which he thanked him genuinely.

"Up from here, you guys are needed to stroll forth all by yourselves, but do not worry, you've to go straight counting your steps, those should be one hundred and fifty for sure & then you'll find yourself to be standing at an intersection; At that point you've to turn left and walk about another fifty steps precisely. And then you've to walk another twenty-five steps after turning right & at last, you'd find the bank just in front of yourselves." Explained Masarah peacefully while caressing Supie's toenail, Sam casted an incredulous look over hcr which meant absolutely – Are you supposing & expecting us to keep this all, in our minds ! To this incredible expression of him as well as his thought, Masarah passed him a nod, which was indeed another beyond belief thing for him but he kept quiet.

"Ok.. But aren't you comin' alon' with us ?" Asked Eveline casually, "No I can't come along as it's necessary for me to head off for to fetch students as the term starts soon." Said Masarah quickly as she heard Eveline "When the term would start ?" Asked Jim blankly "I dunno, I suppose only students know that but do not worry, you'd find many students in Jantinget Elber supermarket then you'd get to know bout it." Masarah responded confidently "Janti-ah what ?" Sam asked plainly "Sam you should listen properly, it's Jantinget Elber supermarket." Eveline replied profoundly while staring at him, Sam ignored her, "Ok, all the best for your term !" She said & climbed up onto the beast & flew back into the tunnel.

# CHAPTER FIVE

# TRUST N TREASURES

"Had you guys ever envisaged this before ?!" Asked Eveline with enthusiasm in her profound voice, "Of course not, Eve." Sam responded back to her excitedly while Jim just beamed back to her.

The triplets set about onto their feet to enter the main gateway with the board at the top, when finally they made themselves to enter, they found many persons moving hither & tither, some of them wore hangings while others were wearing easy coat and jeans. Some individuals were visiting the prettily decorated shops while others were easily staring at them, as they passed they saw attractively adorned merchandise of distinguished stores & boutiques, some of the names of the christened stores were – 'Tindan Brooms', 'Roritoes Robes', 'Caryantha's Books' and 'Walduns Pets'. There were ample number of stores, as far as they could see were only shops, the three children heard an old fogey saying "We can get anything we need, Jantinget Elber supermarket's quite big."

As they ambled past, people observed them attentively and some of them even asked who they were. They told them and kept strolling forth, But as they walked forth, people stared at them with utter curiosity as they had not seen them before.

The triplets whipped off their eyes from them & kept following the clandestine aisle which they were told by Masarah. Finally at half past three they had made it to a lofty silver building. A watchman who wore a tight uniform (shown by his discomfort) was there asleep while snoring loudly but as the three tried to unclose the main gate by touching it, he awoke & yelled fiercely "Hey ! What you children are doing ?" "Can't you view, we're goin' inside ?" Sam said bitterly as he stepped forward towards him but Eveline pulled him back and said softly like an angel "Ah.. Kindly accept my apologies for this cruel behavior of him but he's just a small kid. Actually we want to go inside, we've been sent by Masarah, we know her." "Oh you know OMSOM'S caretaker - Masarah, then there's no necessity for me to block your way, go inside. But first let me check if you people possess any sharp ornament or any stuff like that." Said the watchman politely to her, Sam observed his abrupt change of behavior for a moment unbelievably and whispered in Jim's ear "Why do men change their way of conversing as they begin to talk with a girl ? This is absolutely incorrect." "He hasn't changed his behavior coz of Eveline but coz of Eveline's behavior, see how politely she's communicating with him. She's unlike us." Jim mumbled back to him, due to which Sam looked at him nastily and murmured "Bro, you're on my side, remember." Jim sighed.

The watchman closed his eyes & fluttered his hands ultimately across the jet-black haired girl's physique while mumbling some words in his mouth, he did this with the left two children one after another as he was done doing it with Eveline. "Fine.. You can depart now." The watchman heralded, "Thank you" Eveline said tranquilly.

As they entered the building, they viewed a dozen of counters one after another on which several electronic devices were kept along with library of files arranged officially as well as systematically, particular persons sat there who were busily clicking keys over keys of their keyboards along with their eyes running speedily from one icon to another; They saw many individuals dressed in peculiar dresses which seemed to be their uniforms as almost all of them had themselves wrapped in them, they were carrying cadences in their arms, rushing hurriedly from one counter to another telling significant things to the persons sitting on their unusual comfy seats and they too providing them with edicts over & over as the individuals paused and heard uninterestedly, also mumbling something behind at their backs which obviously seemed cursing as they turned to get hold of their constant instructions.

"Excuse me" Jim called out to a portly chubby man with a bushy beard dressed in white, as he turned towards the blue-haired boy, Eveline rushed forward to hug him to which the man fiercely pushed her but Jim & Sam caught their bestie; Sam yelled out with rage "YOU MAD MAN ! YOU WOULD HAVE HURTED HER SEVERELY !" While Sam kept shouting at the man Jim was asking Eveline if she was all okay while holding her securely in his hands but to his surprise, Eveline stood up sturdily and asked out to the man "Uncle Jack, it's me Eveline ! Your neice ! Don't you remember me ?" The man who was until now neither aware of the girl's identity nor her looks, who was till now responding bitterly to Sam's disrespectful talks, swiveled his head & at the very moment he got a chance to look at the girl to whom he had welcomed with a fierce violent motion, ran forward quickly to take her into his arms & lifted her up and exclaimed joyfully "Evy ! My lovely niece

! How come you're here ?" As the man saw his niece's eyeballs to turn watery he said to her immediately "I am extremely sorry, Evy. I didn't got to know that it was you, I mean I hadn't sighted you, sorry dear." Eveline rubbed her eyes with her fists cutely, as she asked her uncle to put her down, he immediately without any further redo did it as he couldn't hold her any more not because she was heavy or so but because he was himself tackling with his weight.

"No need to apologize, uncle. After all it was my fault, I ran to hug before you could even see me, I shouldn't have reacted like that. I'm sorry." Said Eveline with shame on her face. "Oh my intelligent Evy ! You've quite grown up & matured as well." Her uncle appreciated her apologizing & hugged her tightly which clogged her breath, she was going to choke when two hands pulled her and out came a worried alarming voice "YOU WOULD CHOKE HER OFF MISTER !" That was indeed of Sam & Jim whereas the hands were of a blue-haired boy that was none other than her best friend Jim.

"Who the hell are you two to say that to me ! And who the hell are you to grab away my niece ?!" Asked Uncle Jack furiously to the two boys, "Who the hell are you to ask that !" Said Sam in a raised voice while Jim just glared at him. The man in white was about to respond Sam with a slap when her niece seized his arm and said "Uncle, they're my friends."

The man's expression changed from angry to calm when his niece introduced the two boys with him, as she told the boys that the man was his uncle Jack Faulter who had died eight years ago, they were pretty shocked to hear that but understood the fact when uncle Jack confronted to them that it was just a rumor that was being told to children but the actual reason was that one of his rival had got himself united with one of his family member by bribing & attempted to put him to death but fortunately had failed to do so after which the entire family got frightened from the fact that this incident would turn out to be a cops' call and court case as well and the family members didn't want any trouble so they insisted Jack to leave the house along with his wife and his eleven months old son, to get hold of not only the cops but them too, although in the family there were only seven members – Jack, his wife – Lily, his two years old son – Alex (who was suffering from pneumonia) , his wedded elder sister - Rose, his sister's husband – Ronald, his younger niece – Eveline and his elder niece – Emma.

The man continued hesitantly "After that I thought to pull out my wife, my son and myself as well, from the matter cause your family kept telling us to depart, so I agreed & therefore left along with my small family on the very next day. And-and-" " And- what, uncle ?" Asked Eveline with increasing rage in her voice for her no longer existing parents as she'd not envisaged it to be her own parents.

"And I was the one who told your parents to tell you and your sister that I had died along with my wife and son in an unfortunate road accident, I was the one who instructed your parents to lie to both of yo cause I had known if you and your sister would have been told the truth then you'd be unable to get it and perhaps wouldn't have believed as well." Finished uncle Jack in one go without pausing, Eveline looked at him and stammered bitterly "I-I-I c-can't b-b-bel-believe, m-my o-own p-p-pa-parents d-d-did this wi-with yo-you, I w-w-won't f-f-f-forgive t-t-them f-for d-doing s-such a-a t-th-thing." Eveline's face was damp with the tear droplets dripping down her cheeks, "What's done it's done, Evy" Said uncle Jack while patting at the back of her head passionately acknowledged of her niece's inherited trait of speaking haltingly whenever she turned quite infuriated, however Jim & Sam were unaware of the fact hence were glancing at their best friend with their mouths half opened.

"But where are they anyway and what about Emma ? Where's she ?" Asked uncle Jack hurriedly while looking around hoping to notice someone familiar other than his colleagues but unfortunately got no one's glimpse else than them indeed, Eveline looked at him blankly with no feeling on her face and then turned her face towards her friends then without looking at her uncle said in one breath "They had died." Uncle Jack was taken aback by her words but spoke up immediately when he heard those rude words which came out from his niece's mouth unstoppably "Well, I don't care, what if they did die ? At first, I did care for them for leaving me behind all lonely, I'd shed tears for their demise, But now after hearing you; I think those tears of mine had gone all in vain, I had shed tears for the incorrect individuals, And I even think they deserved it, they got it what they did, in return; as every action has a converse reaction as well." "Evy, they are your parents, you-you shouldn't say such words for your own parents."

"Were, uncle, I had never envisaged that they'd do such-such a sin. Well, they actually demised when I turned five but for me they had left this terra firma at the moment they began conferring you miseries, but I'm too glad that they died as they freed off this earth from their futile burden." Said the girl ruthlessly in one go without flickering her eyes; looking straight into his uncle's eyes, while wiping her moist cheeks she continued ruthlessly "I don't know how many agonies they'd've provided you with, I dunno how many calamities they'd've created for you, I dunno how many times aunt's eyes would have turned watery; but now the only thing I can do is to apologize for all those sins of my demised parents, yes you said very well that they were my parents anyway. Yes unfortunately I did possess a relation with them, they might have forgotten their relation with you but I have not & won't do it either cause I don't intend to be like my ruthless no longer existing parents." Uncle Jack said nothing at this finishing just stood there speechless, kept looking at his knees for sometime when something struck his mind and he asked out loud "What bout my lovely niece Emma ? Where's she ? You didn't tell bout your sister."

For some seconds Eveline couldn't process his words but then after a while she looked at her best friends in the hope of them to respond, to which they too seemed frightened though agreed when they saw Eveline's eyes full of hope; Sam blinked at his buddy to reply but he got it back from him when another time he too winked in return at him, he was quite glad as well as grateful for that his buddy got ready and had admitted his pleasing, Jim spoke out despite Eveline whom uncle Jack was expecting to do so "Ah- She ran away, mister Faulter." Uncle Jack was once again taken aback by the words he had heard, he couldn't manipulate it, he was unable to digest it as it was indeed unbelievable for him to do so, he didn't just consider Emma as his niece but also his all time partner as she was the one with whom he actually was able to confess his torments, his discomforts, his stresses, his emotions, after all everything; she was like his only understandable best friend with whom he used to share every moment of his life as he couldn't do it with his wife because he wasn't intended to let her worry for him. As Emma was ten years older than Eveline so she was the only one who could actually listen and understand uncle Jack.

Uncle Jack remained speechless for some more time, but mustered up guts after about three minutes and asked hesitantly "What do you mean by ran away ? Where has she gone ?" Jim looked at him then responded hesitantly "Ah- Actually.. Mister Faulter.. She-She ran away with Stark, the son of the ugly witch, I mean miss Jones – Our language teacher at the orphanage at which we lived after the death of our respective guardians. Along with us, she was also fed up of that hell and she did tell us that she liked Stark quite a lot but we weren't told about her shirking away with him, ah and we just got aware of that fact on the next day when some students told us of her departure with miss Jones's son on her sixteenth birthday, Tuesday night." Uncle Jack stood stunned as well as silent, his hope of meeting his very favorite buddy vanished as he got to hear all that stuff which came out of the blue-haired boy's mouth, although he was quite a lot disappointed but still he had thoughts of concernment bopping in his head those were just for his elder niece, which compelled him to shout out fiercely "HOW CAN SHE DO THIS ?! MY EMMA ! HOW CAN YOU TRUST A PERSON SO SIMPLY WITHOUT EVEN KNOWING THAT PERSON PRECISELY !" He yelled so hard that the triplets got goosebumps all over their physiques. Knowing her uncle precisely, Eveline was the only person over there who could actually calm down the chubby man with growing rage (revealed by his scarlet red eyes) and she turned out to be that sympathetic person as well.

"But how come you're here, Eveline ?" Asked uncle Jack while breaking the deep silence which had taken place after those sympathetic words of his younger niece which had surely calmed him down.

Eveline without glancing at either Jim or Sam had explained the whole tale of how she and her elder sister were sent to MISERIES TO DELIGHTMENTS (The orphanage) after a few days of their parents' demise which had actually worked out to be the exactly opposite of it's respective label, how she had met Jim and Sam for the very first time when they managed to extricate her from Ason's and his boys' gang's bullying, how she used to cry over her buddies' shoulders for those agonies over agonies she got at that hell from not just the rude bullies over there but also the teachers not excluding the ugly witch and the ruthless caretaker of course, how she was quite a lot delighted at the very moment she got aware of her twelfth birthday's present gifted by Jim through which the three buddies made their escape from the orphanage, how they found out a weird incredible portal via which they made themselves to a entirely dried out plain dimension where they got themselves introduced to an old pretty lady who christened herself to be Masarah, how Masarah made the three's bumps to sit on a peculiar but familiar dragon, how they made themselves to Milantons Mythical World and finally at last, how they got their feet onto the lofty silver building's earth.

When finally Eveline finished her long tale which took approximately fourteen minutes, Jim enabled himself to ask uncle Jack that how come he ended up being there, this question of him was a matter of utter curiosity to not just him but to Sam as well as Eveline too. And Eveline was quite contented to hear the questioning words to come off her buddy's mouth as she had made her throat entirely dried out after the prolonged narrative.

"Well, after our departure, a week would've passed when Alex-d-d-died off cause of pneumonia and after sometime L-L-Lily d-d-did die as well because obviously it was an incredulous trauma for her, she couldn't-ah, you know, even envisage it in any of her nightmares as well." Uncle Jack let out a large tear to fell down from the corner of his left eye on the floor of granite. Eveline was also in the indifferent situation like her uncle while Jim had manifested sorrow as he knew perfectly of how it felt like to lose something or someone on the other hand Sam was impatient for getting furthermore words into and from his ears to his brain of the ongoing tale.

"After that, I struggled to get myself off the trauma of losing not only my sister's family but also my family, And now when I think of it of which I'm compelled of because you people made me to do so, I think I'm actually very hapless that not only did I lose my wife and son but also turned out to be the same for your family as well-" "Absolutely not, uncle... It's not your fault, do not ever come to think of it again in future." Interrupted Eveline in her uncle's continuation, Eveline took hold of her uncle's palms and said slowly while he continued to look over at his knees "I'm extremely sorry for whatever happened with your family just because of my parents, I do understand because I do know epistemology of loss, though not precisely but at least a bit, but do let us know what happened after ah, Alex's & aunt's sad demise ?" Uncle Jack looked at her slowly and while patting at her head's back he responded "I'm glad to know that you've been taught perfectly at that hell or whatever you call it; well.. As I told ago that I struggled to get myself off the trauma but at the end I failed to do so and-and tried to suicide, in order to do so I chose to drown and therefore I tried to find a deep water resource at the nearby woods of my house but haply I found out a portal just like you people did and after that everything went indifferent like yours until miss Masarah managed a job of equity analyst for me at this place where you're standing right now which is referred mostly as the only bank of MMW or as 'TRUST N TREASURES'."

"Well, I wonder where would we need to go to get our accounts transferred ?" Whispered Sam into Jim's ear while making sure that uncle Jack could no longer hear him though somehow he did and did reply as well which was indeed stunning for not only Sam but the other two persons too "Nothing's gonna be terrible or exhausting for you as now you're in my lead so don't worry, I'll be helping out for everything you'd need." Uncle Jack got a glimpse of Sam casting a delighted look over to his best buddy obviously Jim, while saying out those words.

Uncle Jack got something struck once again, which compelled him to thank the two boys and he thanked while beaming brightly, also along with his right hand squeezing the two boys' arms one after another "I'm quite glad that my Evy got friends like you two, thank you so much you twos, both of you always remained beside my Evy, helped her out from the troubles that she faced and even let her make your shoulders drench thoroughly. I dunno how to express this in words but still let me try a bit. I'm really very grateful, seriously I owe to both of you. I don't know if I would ever be able to repay this valuable fav-" "Eve's not just your niece but she belongs to us too as our very best friend, it wasn't just our responsibility to protect her but it's our ultimate content being her buddy and you're embarrassing us by saying such words, mister Faulter." Said Sam, to which Jim agreed by nodding and said out loud to uncle Jack "Of course, kindly don't embarrass us by thanking for what we've done, coz we've done nothing else than what best friends actually do."

Uncle Jack beamed at them while saying to Eveline "Evy you're quite providential that you got friends like these, don't you ever manifest hostility cause getting buddies like these is really arduous." Eveline wondered why uncle Jack had shiny pearls in his eyes while saying, she admitted them to be tears of content in spite of questioning him about it though she wanted to do so but let that thought flew away while responding back to him "Of course not, obviously why would I do so ? D'you consider me a fool or what ?..... Well, I'm actually fortunate enough cause of which I found them six years ago and now I got you as well." Uncle Jack looked at her niece beamingly while talking with the doublets interestedly which had caused Eveline's jealousy to rise up to it's peak.

"You guys know what ? Your friend used to be really childish and mischievous as well, once she had intently but entirely burnt my great moustache saying that I didn't look good with it." This statement of the man had whipped away Eveline's jealousy but had ended her to get argumentative as she said to him that she was just three years old at that time when she did that stuff with him, she had grown up quite a lot since it. "Well she was kinda right. He actually doesn't look handsome with that bushy beard to which he's referring to as a moustache. Right ?" Sam mumbled into Jim's ear to which he got a giggle in return and a nod as well.

"I think we should better get going." Said the two boys together, they glanced at one another then looked away, their thoughts matched really well, but uncle Jack and Eveline'd not even heard as they were engrossed in their argumentation.

Jim and Sam looked at them and again said together "We'd be late for the relocation of our bank accounts, we need to do that as soon as possible then only we'd be able to look for an appropriate venue to live." They both looked at each other stunningly as once again their thoughts had coordinated with one another, they let out a little laughter while glimpsing at uncle Jack and their best friend who were still indulged in their constant argumentation without noticing or even getting bothered by the boys' constant statements.

"I wonder if you both would kindly keep this squabble of yours aside and listen to what we want you to, will be a big help & then only we'd enable ourselves to get to know about the relocation." Said Jim in one go while keeping calm though he had vexed, he'd had enough of that quarreling of the uncle with her niece and did want to silent them with a violent effort of raising his fist and whacking it tightly on a table or just pretending to do so. And this time he might've got his luck on the track which compelled the twos squabbling over there to swivel their heads from one another to him and respond back "We apologize for it." In return he said back to them that it was all fine.

"Okay, now let's get to the point. So you people want to shift your bank accounts, well let me convey some of the very crucial information bout it of which you'd be obviously looking forward to get from this uncle of yours but first let me clarify this to you Jim and Sam that from now onwards, I'll be wanting you two to refer to me as your uncle; no need to be too formal whenever you'd be talking to me, coz it's quite weird for me to be addressed formally by my nephews and also there's no necessity at all." Uncle Jack looked at them carefully as he let out those words of him off his mouth, coincidentally both the boys had not met to any of their uncles before they were sent to MISERIES TO DELIGHTMENTS and had come to know that they didn't even have possess any as well, because of which they were extremely delighted to do what their friend's uncle told thcm to. On the other hand, Eveline's face had turned yellow enough to tell how much she feared of sharing someone's intense affection who was quite close to her heart, although her jealousy had been touching it's peak but she didn't let the boys get it as she knew perfectly after a prolonged period of time they were getting this much attention from somebody other than her, but somehow Jim and Sam got it though Eveline's face was emotion less and they both said at once together unknowingly "Sorry, but I don't want to intrude in between you two, yes I'll absolutely consider and I do consider you as my uncle as you're my best friend's uncle but still I can't do what you want me to. That's just cause I respect my friend's feelings and I don't intent to see my best friend upset by distributing your love that she deserves before me."

Jim and Sam had let out those words so casually that uncle Jack as well as Eveline were actually very shocked to see their confidence, it was like they both had known what the other mate would say. And of course their confidence was appreciating as well as applauding, the two mates looked at each other with little smiles on their faces, their eyes met, like saying to one another 'I didn't know you were going to say that too, bro.' After Eveline had finished with her shocking expression, she allowed her sharp mind to actually get what her buddies had let out their mouths in order to make her free of jealousy, she beamed while saying "As uncle said no need to be formal, so that doesn't just go for, in front of him but in front of me too. Do I look like an idiot to you guys that I'd feel jealousy in such a cheap matter when I didn't even feel it two years past when you two beat me and stood first and second leaving me to stand on the third position ?" Jim and Sam looked at her beaming brightly while letting out words full of compassion once again together but this time knowingly "Oh really Eve ? D'you actually think you can lie to us ?" Eveline looked away without saying anything, she just wanted to hide her tomato red face at that moment, she expected her friends to quarrel with her as they usually did but it was indeed unexpected for her that she ended up being squeezed in their tight arms as they both headed hurriedly towards her to caress her lovingly. Uncle Jack's eyes had turned watery when he saw the triplets in that state which was a matter of utter curiosity to Eveline as he was neither too much emotional nor a pretender although she neither noticed his large shiny pearls nor him wiping them with his shirt's sleeve while managing or struggling to over stretch it to accomplish to do so before getting in anyone's sight.

It was an attestation of the three's profound bond of friendship that when uncle Jack said to them in order to tease them "I'd not want myself to be in such situation for more than a half minute and you three are in that state for more than five minutes, you're making one another to struggle for air I can see it so simply." The three weren't bothered by hearing that or it could be that they hadn't heard it while being getting deep into one another while feeling each other's warmth plus affection as being caressed.

"I'd retch if you'd continue doing it, hey, you three, I'm conversing to you." But the three weren't getting disturbed by being constantly called by a man in white along with a bushy beard, who was just having an intention of teasing them by letting out all those words off his mouth as they were just being involved in a state of endearment, a very long time had passed for them being in that condition (in an actual hug filled with deep content). A great majority of squabbles and disagreements can be resolved simply by breaking down into arms if discussion comes to a violent end according to the triplets although the three were just sharing an act of manifestation of compassion.

Subsequently they let go when they got it back into their minds that they were still left with a lot to do.

"Why did we do it, anyway ?" Asked Sam to his bro while keeping in mind that his words were completely inaudible to Eveline, Jim murmured in return "Why do you suppose I'd be knowing that ?" "I'm not supposing that but I'm damn sure bout it." "I don't think so, in fact I think I noticed, you were the first to head off towards her." Mumbled Jim in return of Sam's surety, Sam was about to reply when Eveline said "Guys, I can see so easily that your lips are handing words over words to each other, well I don't mind though; but I'd be glad if for just now, would you concentrate on what I'm saying ?"

They weren't aware that Eveline had said something when they were indulged in whispering to another.

"Ah, sorry but we didn't hear." Said the two at once. "Not new indeed; by the way I was just asking uncle Jack to tell that significant stuff which he wanted to-" "Oh, I think you'd been looking forward to it." Interrupted uncle Jack as his niece was about to complete. Eveline looked at him and said "Oh yeah, I mean we're also looking forward for it, because it'd be quite necessary for us to know that." "I was neither looking forward nor even expecting him to provide us with the information, coz you know he looks so naive." Whispered Sam to his bro "I do agree with it." Sam got these words in return from him.

# CHAPTER SIX

# KEVIN BANGTHOM

"Okay, so let me begin with a fresh start, yeah so where was I ? Hmm…. Yup, so as I was saying that you'd be looking forward to get some of the very necessary information that how would you enable yourselves to relocate your respective bank accounts from your one & only uncle Jack." Boasted uncle Jack, he continued as he assumed the triplets to be quite curious to hear more although his own niece was the only one who did actually showed some of it, "So for what you want to do, you'll be needed to meet Kevin Bangthom who'd do it for you for now." "Who's that Kevin ? And how would we be able to recognize him ? Asked Jim rapidly as he got to hear some significant things from him for the very first time after about forty five minutes of their meeting "Well, it'd not be arduous for you people to find him as he's the only very handsome person over here after me and also he's a twelve year old boy just like you people are, you'll find him in the gallery, so just go straight from over here and there not so far you'll find him rambling on a clipboard and it'd be comfortable to talk to him unless you talk to him bout something else, so keep in mind to stick to what you want for him to do for you, do not talk bout something else coz he won't like it and would absolutely get ruthless as he always does when someone tries to get to know bout him or converse more than necessity." Finished uncle Jack and that was when he heard his name being called by someone from one of the counter, a man dressed in black with toad like face was there, "Yeah, I'm coming." He responded back to him and then said to the triplets "Okay, I think I'll be needed to go, so let you people head off too and do the work you're needed to and meet me back here in half an hour, well yeah it'd not take a lot of time of yours, for just a simple stuff like that." Said he as he saw the widened eyes of the triplets which he considered had widened because it was quite less time to do such an important work but actually their eyes had widened because they were unable to get it digested that a child was working there. Before they could actually ask that to him, they saw him scurrying over to counter number five.

The three did as were told and began to step forward, on their way they sighted many individuals, some of them indulged in chatting while others were tackling with the cadences in their hands, the triplets wondered why they were not using magical powers as Masarah had boasted that magic could do anything.

"They are real fools that possessing magic they're not utilizing it." Said Sam to Eveline when he enabled his eyes to spot a old man who was about to stumble just because of the overload in his hands while Jim prevented him by tripping, to which he got blessings and a candy in return which looked really peculiar before he got it out of sight by stuffing it in his pocket.

Eveline was really bitter to Sam for not helping the man out and she was constantly passing fierce comments like "Had you not had your hands when that old aged man was about to trip ?!" "I didn't envisaged you to be so much of an idiot who could actually not be kind to an old man." "You know what, you're really very mean." "Sam, you're stu-" "Enough ! Enough Eveline ! I didn't do any crime ! You're treating me as I did one !" Intruded Sam who had got his inner sides entirely vexed up, "Oh yes you've done a crime, for me you are a criminal." Said Eveline, swiveling her head with a jerk while kept strolling forth with the twos, Sam replied back who'd got really annoyed of her "Fine ! It's a crime for you madam but not for us or the others, so keep your mouth shut !" "Who the hell are you to shut up my mouth !" Yelled Eveline with growing rage in her sturdy voice which still had a bit of softness in it just for the sake of their friendship. " For your very kind information I am your friend unfortunately ! And kindly keep your voice a bit down." Said Sam who himself had his voice in his control, "I won't ! You heard me, I won't keep my voice down ! What would you do ?!" Demanded she with her voice going up a lot more than before "I'll cast a spell on you with which it would be impossible for you to even unclose your mouth." Said Sam as fast he could, after hearing those rude words of his friend. "Oh really ? You have not even got yourself admitted in that school and you're talking about jinxing me." Said Eveline in return while letting out a laugh off her mouth. Meanwhile Jim was unable to get himself off his vexation which was growing as more ruthless words of his friends made their way from his ears to brain.

Finally at last he spoke up while controlling his volume "It's suffice ! Stop it ! It's like I can't even envisage a day, oh, not a day but an hour of mine without you two squabbling with one another ! Can't you two give it a rest to yourselves ?! Your brains would be frustrated and even fed up by giving you such rude thoughts to shout out for each other.

And Sam can't you zip lock your lips ? Can't you manifest some maturity by not responding back ? But no you keep replying in return like a fool coz whenever Eveline says to you something which turns out to be correct mostly, your insides begin to burn, right ?!"

These words of him had not just ended up the verbal fight of them but unfortunately had mutilated Sam mentally; for the following way of theirs Jim was really grateful to hear nothing coming out of his friends' mouths else than comments about the shabby walls of the place or the people who were hurrying.

"Where is that Kevin ? Mister Faulter had told us to make it to the gallery and we're here." Said Jim as he glanced around to notice no one young enough to be a twelve year old boy. After which he heard someone saying at his and his friends' back "What's the matter to call my name ?" As he & his friends turned, he and Sam were stunned as uncle Jack was really correct about the boy's looks, he was really very handsome. A boy with dark black hairs, brown eyes, baby pink-colored lips, a sturdy physique and a clipboard in his hands.

But the boy's eyes were filled with hatred as he spoke up to them "Are you people deaf ?" Sam and Jim stepped forward but Eveline pulled them back by snatching their shirts and whispered to them "If you'll gape at somebody like you did right away without responding to him or her then what do you expect that person to say to you ?" Kevin was about to move from there when Eveline spoke up confidently "We want our bank accounts to be transferred and we were told to meet you in order to get that done." Kevin turned towards her, saw her from head to her feet and said with no feeling on his handsome face "Well in that case, you've come to the right person indeed. Come with me."

The three followed him and after a while they made themselves enter into a big office which was adorned with greyish black-colored curtains, four vases in there which had the same colored flowers too which were kept on the top of small shelf with only books, a big shelf with quite many folders arranged systematically with perfection and at last a crystal clear table made up of pure glass with a comfy seat on the other side made just for an official person or an officer and two comfy seats on the side where the four were standing.

"Wait a minute." Said Kevin and he hurried off to close the door while the triplets noticed a label kept on the table with 'Sompeodar Bangthom – The Manager' written on it in italic font. "I think this is his father's workroom." Whispered Jim "And perhaps this job too." Said Eveline quietly back to him as Kevin emerged in front of them and said "What're your account numbers ?" "We don't know." The three replied instantly "You people don't know your own bank account numbers, hmm, seems like you're not considered trustworthy by your parents." Said Kevin while smirking, Jim was about to speak when Eveline spoke up confidently "Absolutely not, but it wasn't a suitable age to get to know things like bank account number." Kevin glared at her then said "Whatever; well if you people aren't aware of your account numbers then I'll be needed to do some more stuff too." The triplets observed him moving towards at Sam and saying out to him "Give me your hand." "Why ?" Asked he, to which the boy said rudely "Do as I say." Sam murmured something to himself which was for sure some abusive words then placed his palm onto Kevin's palm, he noticed him whispering something to himself which was surely a spell with which he was finding his account number.

"Ok, now give me your hand." Said Kevin to Jim, "Did you get to know my account number ?" Asked Sam when the handsome boy placed his hand onto another handsome boy's hand, this question of Sam didn't bother Kevin and he ignored him, again he mumbled a word to himself and then at last he said "All well, now give me your hand." This time this was said for none other than Eveline as no one was left other than her.

She stepped forward and gave her hand to him but this time he didn't murmur anything instead he looked at her shockingly and tightened his grip, obviously this was strange for her although she didn't say anything as she considered it to be a prime part of the occult he was performing, Kevin didn't speak a single word just kept staring at Eveline, it could be easily seen by his expressions that many questions had erupted in his mind which were causing him to ponder as he gazed at her, it was like he'd got a thought which was really incredulous to him. This continuous gaping of him was neither troubling Eveline nor her friends but his clutch kept tightening itself which was causing discomfort to Eveline, it was not that she was feeling pain as she was so sturdy although not much in the case of mental strength.

Subsequently he released her hand from his strong hold as soon as he realized the surroundings, when he got back to his senses that he was still under the sight of three pairs of eyes which were watching him incessantly, but absentmindedly to what he had done at that moment, he didn't get her account number after which he said blankly to her, this time his voice had a bit of docility "Ah, I-I didn't get your account number, ah, let me try once-once more." Eveline without any redo obediently placed her delicate hand on his while Jim and Sam just gaped at the handsome boy unbelievably. This time, Kevin casted a spell whisperingly, let go her soft hand instantly as he was done and then went near the table, seized the only tablet which was kept on it and began to move his index finger over it while keeping it away from the reach of the eyes of the two boys over there.

After about ten minutes he said out loud "The shifting has been done, your respective bank accounts have been transferred from your respective banks to Trust n Treasures. The only thing left, is to provide appropriate labels to them, so tell me what names you want to give to your bank accounts ?" The three gaped at him incredibly as it took him only ten minutes to do it. Sam was the first to speak with enthusiasm in his sturdy voice "Sam Mahongthan's rich world." Kevin stared at him, let out a little laugh which Sam didn't notice haply as if he'd done so then again a quarrel would've erupted, then Jim said "Jim Sueruds bank account." Kevin typed it on the vacant input box of his respective bank account then he looked at Eveline without any ruthlessness on his face which he had for the boys "Diligence" Said Eveline as she got to read Kevin's eyes which were asking her what title she would like to provide her bank account. Not just Kevin looked at her blankly but Jim & Sam also had their eyeballs on her which were simply asking her for a reason or a convincing argument behind that purpose. They seem to say to her that there were quite many fancy names out there in the universe that could be given despite of such monotonous name, their eyes asked her on which grounds she was christening her account 'Diligence'. Eveline didn't answer but she understood what their eyes were saying to her. Kevin fumbled then typed it down too like he had done two times before.

"All good, your accounts have been christened as well. Now whenever you need to borrow finances or have any significant work related to your bank accounts then just meet mister Sompeodar Bangthom, well you'd have got who is it anyway, my father." Said Kevin with no ruthlessness in his voice as he was gaping at Eveline. "It means this job is not yours, right ?" Asked Sam interestedly, Kevin without turning his head answered at once with ruthlessness in his voice "Yes, it's not mine." "Well, we better go now." Said Jim as he looked at his wrist watch which had struck quarter to six, Eveline nodded but not Sam though all three left the office, leaving Kevin all alone.

"Why did you christen it 'Diligence' ?" Asked Sam while keeping distance between him and Jim, as the triplets made their way from between the hustling-bustling people still having loads of cadences in their trembling arms, "Wha-oh that, well basically I thought it'd take diligence for me to fill up my account with money, as if I won't do donkeywork then I would never be able to fill it up with that on which this whole world works." Replied she smartly "Smart thought, Eve." Appreciated Jim following Sam who'd praised by saying "Good thinking !"

Suddenly they heard an alarming voice from their behind which shouted out to them "Watch out !" When they looked back, they had felt like their hearts would come out of their maws any moment, they were dumbfounded horrifyingly as they had their eyes on the many wooden planks those were neither carried by someone nor were fluttering but those highly weighted wooden planks were about to crush Jim when an arm reached out to clutch his arm to pull him hard enough to prevent him from getting mashed up like a potato.

The two arms were holding Jim's hands securely as well as sturdily though it looked like they were being wrapped around his arms, the two's physiques curtailed & curtailed and finally stopped with a jerk because they had been smacked by the wall but haply were not scraped, no blood no scratch no wound, at all nothing had happened to the two to everyone's astonishment who were watching this menacing spectacle with their hands on their maws and who were expecting the two to be in a pool of blood although luckily their expectation did not become reality. And that was when everybody over there had their eardrums burst due to the heavy thumping sound made by the planks which had smashed onto the granite floor and were now turned to pieces.

"Are you two alright ?" Asked out a worried voice to the two, when the two looked over to see no one else than their very best friend Eveline along with her watery eyes with the fear of losing her friends into them, Jim and Sam who were lying on the floor side-by-side got to their feet immediately and answered together cheerfully "All well, Eve." Sam glimpsed at Jim then looked away.

Jim looked at Sam and hugged him tight then let go and said to him with the same most appealing smile on his face "Thanks bro, if you'd not saved me then I'd have been squashed and perhaps wouldn't have been standing in front you-" "Nothing could happen to Jim until his bro is alive." Interrupted Sam while looking away, Jim beamed, Eveline asked him "Jim, where's your bracelet ?" Jim looked at his wrist anxiously and stood there dumbstruck with the horror of losing his mother's last mark. "Perhaps somewhere here." Said Sam who was still looking away, Jim without any redo began to search for it with all his hopes but was unable to find it, he thrashed his fist onto the floor while squatting and said to himself "I'm stupid ! I'm the biggest foolish of this universe, it was my mom's one and only thing left after her demise." He had whacked his fist once or twice when Eveline caught his hand from which blood was dripping down persistently, she said alarmingly "Jim, stop ! Stop being rude to yourself ! It's not your fault at all." Jim looked at her, pulled his hand from her grip and said to her "No ! It is my mistake ! I'm an idiot that I lost my-; Sam, I called you fool not so long ago, but you know what, I'm sorry for it cause I think, not you but I'm the biggest foolish person of this whole world." Jim broke down entirely into his friend's arms while Sam kept looking at the girl hopefully who had Jim in his arms, he was expecting her to calm him down but she herself was handling optimistic looks to him, Sam was left with no option and leapt up to his friend maintaining suffice distance between him & Jim, he said "Jim, Eve's right, it's not your fault; but wait, you didn't check in that office, did you ?" Jim looked at him with half opened mouth then leaving the two behind, he ran towards the office as he heard them shouting out to him "We're waiting for you here !"

He panted as he had his hand onto the doorknob, but subsequently he was unable to turn it as he'd heard some whispers from the other side which according to him were made by Kevin (As he got to hear his voice only) "How could it be possible ?" "Dad had told him that I'd be unable to find her." "I was in her search from the moment I had had my feet on this earth." "Is she the one or have I misunderstood her to be the one ?" "But neither I'm eighteen nor she is, well I think she's not because she also looks too young to be that and... I think she's twelve just like me; so then how could it be not impossible that we met so early ?" "Had I misheard grandpa ?" "But if she is the one then there's a necessity for me to keep a look on her although I'm needed to scrutinize once more in order to get a confirmation and also before throwing my precious time into the bin." "But wait, I'm not aware of her name. She wouldn't have gone too far, let me ask her out." With these words out his mouth, Kevin dashed out of the office & without letting his motile eyeballs to go anywhere, he headed straight forward unknown of the fact that Jim wasn't so far standing just beside him.

Jim for some seconds wasn't able to get the stuff he'd heard down his throat but then his mum's bracelet came running back to his clever mind and compelled him to push the thoughts aside for sometime and he ran inside the workroom without anyone's consent though there was nobody to ask for it. He searched and searched unless he got it back in his hands after which he kissed it adoringly and said to it while hooking it back precisely in the way his mother had done for the very first time that had unfortunately become her last time too "I'll never lose you again, I promise this to you mom."

When he made it back to his friends he saw Kevin conversing casually with them, the things he had heard came rushing back to his brain while he gaped at him who was saying "I'm so embarrassed for my behavior, I apologize for it, I hope you people will pardon me." "Of course, I forgave you Kevin. Didn't you Sam ?" "Well, if he's actually sorry for being ruthless then I would not mind forgiving him." Answered Sam to Eveline's question as he observed Jim who had suspicious expressions on his face while gazing at Kevin. "And what bout you, Jim ?" Asked Eveline as she swiveled her face from Sam to him in the hope that he'd also pardon him but to her surprise he contrasted as she heard him "Well, is it mandatory for me to do that ? No, right ? So, I'll think about it later." These careful contrasting words of Jim had not just pushed Sam and Eveline into utter confusion but also had forced Kevin's rudeness to come rushing backwards to him, for him to be back like before he was, but this time only for the blue-haired boy – Jim Sueruds. Kevin said ruthlessly "I don't care, if you don't." He continued while turning his head from Jim from to the other two "But I'm glad that I got some very intelligent friends, well I got your name as you christened your account with it but what's your name, lady ?" Eveline who was unable to take her eyes off Jim just because of his weirdness, somehow did so and said to Kevin "Eveline Guitonnet, Kevin." "Very nice name indeed !" Exclaimed Kevin then he continued "But don't you think it's a bit too long ? So will it be fine if... I christen you ? I mean, a name with which I can only refer to you." Before Eveline could answer in affirmative as she wanted to, Jim spoke ruthlessly "No need" Kevin ignored him then asked once more "Will it be okay, Eveline ?" This time Eveline spoke up before Jim could "Do you think that I'll deny ? Obviously not, after all you're our friend. Right Sam ?" Sam noticed Jim giving him fierce looks then said "Ah, I dunno, I mean Jim doesn't agree with-" "Ohhhh I'm not talking bout Jim, I'm talking bout us, the two of us. Can't we have more friends else than him ? Yes we can have so therefore, we do agree to be your friends and you can call me by any name you want, Kevin." Intruded Eveline bitterly.

Jim stared at her unbelievably as he could not believe that his best friend's conversation about him which always had words full of generosity for him, which always had tales of his saviors, which never had his mistakenly did misdeeds, which never ever had ruthless talks of him, was now no longer like before.

Sam was also in utter shock that their best friend was no longer just theirs, their best friend who always had irking vocabularies off of her larynx whenever somebody spoke something thought-provoking for her buddies had turned out to have become ruthless for them.

Kevin smirked while gaping at the two dumbass (according to him) as Eveline told Sam that if he didn't want to be Kevin's friend then it would be all okay but she did not need the two's assent whether she could be or not. Jim and Sam widened up their eyes then looked at each other with their eyes saying to one another 'Pinch me, I can't trust my eyes.' "I'll call you Evans, ain't nice ?" "It is really nice." Responded Eveline to Kevin as she grinned cutely but suddenly they heard a voice calling out to them, when the three along with the fourth one turned back they viewed mister Faulter standing in front of them who'd just said "So here you are and I thought that you left."

Uncle Jack looked at Kevin then with his hand out towards him said to him "Hey Kevin ! We met after about a long time." Kevin at first didn't want to do so but when he sighted the only girl over there through the corners of his eyes, unintentionally and uninterestedly had his hand out and nastily did the handshake. Eveline asked "How come, uncle Jack ? I know Kevin does his job ever so often in his dad's absence but then too don't you two get to meet every so often as you both work here whatsoever ?" Before mister Faulter could answer, Kevin replied politely "We don't get time for that, as we two are busy at all times." Uncle Jack was really stunned to Kevin's politeness for the very first time as the feeling he every so often had was just savagery or rage (due to his private reasons) Kevin continued "But Evans, how do you know mister Faulter

?" Eveline without any lateness responded cheerfully "Coz he's my uncle, Kevin." "What ? Mister Faulter is your uncle ?" Asked Kevin blankly "Yes Kevin, Evy is my dearest niece." Said uncle Jack happily while patting at his niece's back.

"Well, mister Faulter I think we should depart as we're still left with many things to get done like getting a house at rent-" "Do you think that I'll let you children live at rent when I'm here ?" Jim was about to speak when he was once again interrupted by uncle Jack "You'll be living along with me at my place. I'd not listen any of your excuse in it. Now you'd be needed to get your stationary, uniforms, new school bags etc.. so just go and get yourself done with the shopping, here have these, I think this'd be enough for it so head off and purchase all of it." Uncle Jack handed them three wallets full of currency notes and coins, when they took hold of them, Jim and Sam said together after looking at one another affirmatively "Sorry but we can't take." Uncle Jack looked at them then said "I've got it from the moment I'd seen you at first that you both are self-dependent but I did tell you that I'm your uncle so there's no need to be formal-" "You are our uncle but I don't think it would be right for us to-" "I told you not to be formal in front of me earlier too; but I know you won't accept, so let you consider it a loan and repay it later in future when you would've got a job." Intruded uncle Jack in Jim's intruding, "But uncle-" "Oh Evy not you too now !" Said uncle Jack as he heard Eveline about to begin on the same topic but in her case. Uncle Jack continued "You're my only niece and also my family, how could you expect me to take it back from you ? I'd take it from the boys cause I know they'd not take it if I'd not consider it as a loan-" "It is a loan, mister Faulter." Interrupted Jim. Uncle Jack began to speak "See Evy, anyways, you people should head off to Jan-" "Tinget Elber supermarket, right ?" Completed Sam cheerfully "Yeah, absolutely; you're needed to head off there as soon as possible cause it'd be on it's way to get closed, I mean it's closing time is half past eight and you'd need quite much time to buy all of your stuff." Said uncle Jack as he sighted his analog watch which was striking quarter past six. "Sorry for it but I can't accompany you with your shopping cause I've got some clients with whom my meeting was appointed from past two weeks and I've been delaying from many days but I couldn't delay it anymore, I hope you understand. Anyways, meet me at the entrance when you'd be done, I'll pick up you people from it. Then we'll head off straight to my location." These were the last words of uncle for now as the four sighted them getting vanished among the hustling-bustling people.

"Are you taking admission in OMSOM, Evans ?" Asked the only boy over there who referred to her by that name, "Not just me but these two too." Answered she while fluttering her hand from Sam to Jim, "Well whether they're getting admitted or not, that does not matter to me at all; all that matters to me is you are getting admitted." Kevin mumbled to himself keeping his voice really down so as to avoid it getting heard by anybody but haplessly (or should be said haply in the blue-haired boy's accordance) Jim heard him which pushed him in profound confusion as well as rage neither because he had any lovely-emotions for his best friend nor because he had any jealousy for her (which he would not be having either as he didn't has any feelings) that was just because he possessed an ultimate and strong relation of friendship with her from a prolonged period of time and he couldn't help himself from getting anxious for his best friend when he had heard some really thought-provoking words off a stranger's maw not so long ago; but he did not ask Kevin about his words.

"Well, we need to hurry up." Said Jim with the determination of telling his friends what he'd heard Kevin saying, "Yes but we aren't aware of our term's books as we haven't got admission yet, first we need to get it." Said Eveline rapidly, then Kevin said to her "No it's not like that Evans. In OMSOM you're needed to get your stationary subsequently you'll get yourself admitted." "What ? It's too weird." Said Eveline as it was unlike any other school in their dimension. "Well, yeah it is weird for you people as you're from a different world but in MMW it is not, in fact I consider it to be advantageous as when you would get all of your school stuff and when you'd go to them to ask for admission then they can't deny as you can tell them that you've already bought the things." Said Kevin boastingly, Sam asked him while winking at Jim "Not even when the seats are full ?" Kevin stared at him and unintentionally responded "Of course not, don't be ridiculous, they'd only provide you with it when they're not out of seats."

"But then also we dunno what stationary we need to get." Said Eveline anxiously while staring at Jim in the hope that he'd be sorry for the words that he'd let out of his maw for Kevin but she was again disheartened to see no sorrow on his face "Well, that's not a trouble at all, as I'm aware of all the books, here take this Evans." Said Kevin as he handed her a small whitish rectangular-shaped piece of paper, as she took it in her hands, she ran her eyes over it, she saw a very pale note with very thin straight borders and a list inside the borders which was the christenings of six books along with the christenings of their authors which were written beautifully in cursive handwriting in licorice ink with fountain pen.

Let's get GMK by Emma Clairs
Wonders of Science by Liliyan Peteruts
Mathema by Ron Saneiro
Around the globe by Los San Mttae
Occult with Error by Dan Te Lao
Love your tongue by Dolly Teeturs

"Have you bought them ?" Asked Eveline as her eyes moved back to Kevin's face from the note, Kevin answered as quickly as he could while beaming "No not yet I'll buy later but you can have this as I won't encounter any problem in getting another list." Eveline without any redo said to him "But why don't you come along with us ? It'll be fun if we all would do the shopping together, will it be not ?" Kevin's eyes were shining, it could be simply manifested from his face expressions that he actually wanted to join them or just her (according to Jim) though he denied her offer, when she questioned him about the cause for doing so, he told her that he could not leave the bank in the absence of his father as he'd assured him to do his job in his place till he gets back from the business tour.

"Well bad luck, right ? But do not worry I'll see you on the first of may as the term starts from it." Said the black-haired boy, he continued as he began to stroll backwards with his very handsome face still at the jet black-haired girl "And yeah one more thing, other than books, in your stationary haul you're needed to purchase pencil, eraser, three pens of three different colors of your own choice, error corrector, geometry box, dissection box, a rough notebook, a writing-tablet, twelve hardboard portfolios, six full-size packets of A4 sized sheets, permanent as well as temporary markers, sketch pens, crayons, acrylic paints, brushes with different strokes, a palette..... Hmm did I miss anything ? I don't think so, well, that would be all. See you on the first of may Evans !" And he got himself out of the triplets' sight.

"I consider it to be an endless list." Commented Sam as Kevin vanished in the crowd, Eveline said "Well, yeah it was a bit-" "Bit ? Are you kidding me Eve ? That wasn't just a bit. I don't even remember the first thing he mentioned." "But I do." Said she cheerfully. "Everyone's not alike you, Eve." Said Jim in an appreciating manner but Eveline took it in the other way "You mean to say, I'm a special child." Said she fiercely, Jim widened up his eyes and said rapidly "No I didn't mean that-" "I got it what you meant." Said she before he could complete his sentence. "I know why you behaved with Kevin like that, you are jealous that I've made a new friend, so just because of this jealousy of yours you did that." Continued she bitterly "Eve, it's not like that, you're totally free to have as many friends as you want else than me but I just thought him to be peculiarly weird, I mean his behavior with us at first was so cruel and then suddenly he realized that he did wrong and started apologizing, don't you think it was so strange of-" "Not at all ! You think that ! But my thinking can't be same as yours at all times ! So if you could do me a favor then please whenever I'd be conversing with him and if he asks you something though he won't as I'll make him aware of this ruthless behavior of yours but, but if by chance he converses with you then kindly talk in the way you do with me and Sam." Intruded she; Jim was about to speak when she spoke up bitterly "And one more thing don't you dare to talk rubbish bout him coz for your very kind information he has turned out to be friend for me and you know very well that I can't and won't listen nonsense about my friends." Jim said "For y-o-u-r very kind information, I am a best friend of yours and I don't wanna compete with him cause you know why, I and you've been friends from an extensive period of time whereas you have got him not more than some minutes ago." "Then also he is my friend and I won't bear contempt for him." Said she mercilessly then without letting the blue-haired boy say anymore word she said to him furiously "It'd be better if you stay out of our matter, it'd be better if you don't poke your nose into our discussions, and it'd be better if we neglect talking bout him in our conversations coz you'll disrespect him unreasonably and I won't tolerate such ridiculous sort of stuff of yours." Jim sighed and resisted his temptation of spilling rage off his chest because he knew if he'd do so then the situation would go wild as well as obstreperous to handle. Meanwhile Sam was just not able to manipulate his friend Eve's cruel words for her own best buddy. He considered a change in topic would not worsen the situation and it didn't do so either, in fact it turned out to be helpful.

"Let us be off to that market cause it's already half past six." Said Sam as he took hold of Jim's wrist to look over at his watch which was indeed striking 6:30 in the evening.

# THE INCONCEIVABLE VALOR

As the triplets made their way out of Trust n Treasures, they set about onto the terra firma to made themselves to plunge into a bookstore labeled as 'Caryantha's Books' and they set into it as well.

Wherever their eyeballs went they were not amazed to view shelves full of books, books & only books for people of every age. Tomes, novels, storybooks, biographies, autobiographies, schoolbooks, magazines, hardcovers, paperbacks, anthologies and many more. Not to their surprise, except for them there were many youngsters along with their mommies and daddies though not all of them were having their parents around. The triplets eyes were curtailing in awe as it was a spectacular array for them to see such a vast bookshop. There in it were nearly nineteen to twenty bookracks of about 144 inches. The dilapidated walls were unable to get in view because of the stacks though they weren't mattering to the customers.

There were sections for dissimilar books which were manifested by the medium sized panels with the type of books to be kept in that particular area. 'Wonders Of Horrors – For books accounting macabre and are gruesome.', 'Fantasy Myths – For books accounting occulted historic incidents.', 'Magnificent Technologies – For books accounting latest innovations and high-tech advancements made in MMW.', 'Kiddo's Stuff – For books accounting fairytales, wizardries and witchcrafts.', 'Happening Hither & Tither – For magazines and paperbacks accounting current affairs across the globe.', 'Ultimate Romances – For books accounting romantics and infatuated youths' accounts.', 'OMSOM'S Schoolbooks – For books accounting knowledge for students of MMW's one and only school; just for academic purpose.'.

As the triplets' spotted that plank, they ran towards that section and were surprised to see quite many youngsters over there looking for their grade's books, though the triplets didn't know their grade but still they knew which books they'd be going through with through their term and the jet black-haired girl was really grateful to the black-haired handsome boy for lending them the note but this act of him had also baffled her as how did he know in which grade the three would be moving to; though the girl didn't let herself to get mystified a lot as she considered that he got it by their ages, there'd to be a rule in the magical school that children would be sorted into the classes according to their respective ages or else a statement would've been passed by the principal of it otherwise Kevin would not have been so certain – She told herself.

"Hey ! Here is the 'Wonders of Science', let me take three." Cried out Sam joyfully as he took three copies of it, "Have you people got any books ?" Asked he cheerfully "Not yet, still looking." Responded Eveline while scrutinizing each academic book's name scrupulously. After a while the three cried out in joy together, they looked at one another, their eyes asking to each other's eyes which book you got. "Well, I got 'Let's get GMK'." Said the jet black-haired girl happily following Sam & Jim. "I got 'Around the globe'." "And I got 'Occult with Error'." The triplets took three each of the books they found. "Two more left." Said Sam as he tackled with the burden of six really loaded books in his hands, while letting out really slowly in order to avoid a new squabble along with his studious friend. "I dunno how I'd enable myself to come to grips with these volumes." After a while Jim found the rest two too & grabbed three each of them also, Jim who was handling more weight (as he had nine very hefty books) than Sam was not getting bothered by it, not even a stressful screw was on his forehead, and that was just because he was pondering about something else or perhaps something in the past (not very long ago) was coercing his mind to care about it but he didn't let it manifest that there were some thoughts hopping in his mind which were really bothersome to him.

"How much for these ?" Asked Eveline to the man standing at the counter who looked really very young, and indeed he was too, the triplets got to know that when a customer asked him how many years old he was and in return he replied that he had turned nineteen on the recent 31$^{st}$ of march while vanishing two white rats which were fighting on the floor with each other out of his sight by shouting out loud "Vanisho !" While pointing both of his palms at them and out emerged a red ray of light and it hit them together as their little arms were being wrapped around one another in order to murder each other. It could be easily manifested from the young man's face that he did that just because of his fear of rats although the rats looked very pretty with the white fur and their fight had turned out to be very much enthusiastic to Eveline that she had let out a "So adorable !" Off her voice box. But on the same time she was really amused as well disappointed when the rats were no longer visible. She was amused because once again she had sighted an occult and disappointed of course she had turned because she could no longer view the cute rats. But her friends hadn't shown much astonishment this time as both of them had made up their minds and thought that they had to become usual to these small magical events as they were no longer in their dimension, they were in an entirely different dimension, they were in a magical world.

"Six hundred brontads" Said the man as he looked at the loads of the books the three partners had placed on the counter's oak wood table, the girl had let these words of the man to propel her sharp brain into sturdy mystification as she was baffled why she did she hear brontads as an alternative of dollars. She exchanged confused looks with Sam when Jim took out two notes off his wallet, he answered them when the two gaped at him mystifyingly "What ? This is a different dimension. Don't you guys remember ? So the currency would be unlike ours." The two heard him and their mystified looks vanished as well as they too took out two notes each from their wallets and handled the shopkeeper the total amount – Six Crisp notes with '100 Brontads' labeled on the top left corner of each of them. "Thank you, come again !" The three heard the young man shouting after them as they headed off the store while grasping the three average sized jute bags each with six hefty books.

The next shop they went in was 'Roritoes Robes', in there the triplets saw numerous gigantic wardrobes though the store was not as vast as the bookstore was, it was a boutique with apparels hanging on holders everywhere, some of them looked hand-knitted while others looked readymade but still all of the designs were pretty. In fact the previous store was still adorned with LED moonlightings, little pots with dandelions etc. But this boutique neither did need any single thing of them nor did it had space for such an elaboration.

"How can I help you ?" Asked the same old fogey they had seen when they were in the search of 'Trust n Treasures'. The triplets asked him if they could get school uniforms in there. To this question of theirs the old fogey insisted them to wait in there for sometime as the trial rooms were all full, when they'd be vacant then they could also try out the various sizes. The jet black-haired girl asked him where the school robes were to be kept as they wanted to see the uniform. The old fogey without any lateness went towards an extensive cupboard and took some clothes in his arms, turned and went to them. He said to the two boys while handing them some unwrinkled robes "Well, these are the last pieces, all the uniforms for boys would be out of stock after these, I hope these will fit you." As their eyes went by, they saw two light brown-white colored shirts, two pairs of dark ebony colored full pants, two chestnut colored ties along with dark ebony colored stripes on it drawn in a zigzag method, two pairs of chestnut colored socks and at last two dark ebony colored belts with a smart design of maple leaf in the middle of it (in the tying portion), that was the school's monogram.

"What bout me ?" Asked the jet black-haired girl politely while glancing at the dresses amusedly as they looked too good if to be wore. The old fogey told her to look for her size in the same cupboard as soon as possible because dresses for girls had though not gone out of stock but still weren't quite many.

She ran towards the massive cupboard and was not surprised to see nothing changed in the uniform else than the replacement of dark ebony colored pants with the same colored miniskirt and same colored stockings as an alternative of chestnut colored socks. She got her size after rejecting a numerous dresses which took her too long due to which the boys were really very annoyed of her as they had also tried up their uniforms which fortunately or as luck would have it, fitted them perfectly and also they'd managed to do the payment of their dresses during when their best friend was still indulged up in getting her size, Jim and Sam would have left the boutique but haply (just for the sake of the boys' best friend's tardiness whenever she got herself into physical appearance enhancers or apparels stores) the old fogey got themselves busy with him in conversation so as to prevent them from departing without their partner which was absolutely very benevolent of him.

"Come again !" Once again they heard as they seized their bags and departed off. The robes were more exorbitant than the books though it's neither a thing to be fascinated about nor to be discussed about in the blue-haired handsome boy's accordance as he considered it to be certainly obvious and perhaps that is why he did not involve himself in his two best friends' korero on the listless topic.

When the three had done it (shopping) completely after the hundreds or should be said millions (which could be easily said of course by getting a look of Sam's fatigue and also his over dramatic body language), they were dying to ease up and to throw the many hefty bags due to which their arms were in extreme agony therefore they departed straight for the entrance of Trust n Treasures and saw uncle

Jack already present there whose cheerfulness had faded away just because of the tiredness with which his mind as well as his body was dealing so bad though he managed to greet the triplets through a weak smile by clutching it too hard from deep inside his soul in order to hide the tediousness though he was unable to do so and he got it when the triplets asked him adoringly if he intended for any help in strolling forth then he could absolutely ask for it to them. To which he just smiled weakly although he wanted to respond back but his maw didn't support because of constantly speaking in his meeting, this fact was told by Jim to his friends in a whispering etiquette when they were nearly about to approach the man once again to ask him the same question.

The triplets didn't let anything to spill off their tongues when they were strolling along with the exhausted man who himself wasn't in the state to speak anything as well and hence didn't say anything like the three. It would have taken them almost twenty minutes to make it to a very pale apartment which was not too tall, when they entered they were amazed to see the ground floor wholly deserted, not a single individual was there, which gave birth to an insecure feeling in their minds as at their orphanage nobody did sleep until the caretaker's hands would have clutched a lean piece of cane at sharply half past ten. And here Jim's and others' (whoever had) watches had only struck quarter past nine, "Found it extremely peculiar, right ?" Finally the man tackled with his maw to ask that out to the triplets who looked at him with an obvious expression though didn't reply as they heard the man's voice had echoed heavily. "I also found it to be that when I met this place for the very first time at midnight. Well don't worry bout it cause there's a rule in here followed by everybody whoever lives here, that is, everybody who tends to get a flat over here has to make it to it before half past eight." The exhausted man finished weakly as the four strolled forth towards the escalator viewing nothing than a series of rooms' closed doors and bright lights. The apartment looked quite neat although there was a strong odor of burnt milk which antagonized Eveline really very much that she was coerced to press her hand hard enough on her nose which really left imprints when she finally let go her nose preventing it from getting suffocated, and that was when the four felt to move up which wasn't peculiar though as they were in the lift and the button with six written on it had been pressed just a few seconds ago.

When they got off the lift, the man instructed to the four to stay with him as he sighted some drunkards who were simply roaming which definitely shouted out loud that they were all idle. "What else would they do ?" Commented Sam whisperingly in Jim' left ear.

And when the four were just passing by them, the drunkards noticed mister Faulter unclearly and ignored but when they got a blurred vision of the three children walking along with him, they slowly moved towards them, blocked their way, to which the four didn't react much just glared at them unblinkingly, turned to take another pathway but once again they were being blocked by the same drunk people.

One of them while glancing at the triplets said to mister Faulter "Seems like you've brought new guests, won't you introduce us to them ?" Mister Faulter glared at him for some seconds then said to them furiously "None of your business. Leave our way." "How can it be not our business ? We won't leave your way unless you tell us who they are." Said the third man who was continuously gazing at

Eveline unblinkingly. He made a step towards her and said to her "Extremely beautiful, I'd absolutely want myself to introduce to you." Mister Faulter without any redo placed his hand steadfastly on his niece's shoulder while she was clutching her friends' shirts, her uncle said out loud to the same man who'd stepped forward towards his niece "I said leave our way ! Don't compel me to call the owner !"

"Call him ! We aren't afraid of him." Said the first man while stepping forward, the second man seemed to be critically pondering about something but said after a while following the third man who had agreed with the first one "Yes we're not !", "Well, we can leave your way on just one condition." The other two men stared at him incessantly while the three gaped at one another when mister Faulter asked him furiously "What condition ?"

"Well, if you will lend this extremely pretty girl to us for just a couple of hours then we will certainly let you people go." This time Eveline had grabbed her friends' hands not because of fear but because her friends were being vexed up since the moment the punk rascals had begun to talk nonsense and being knowing her friends perfectly she had grasped their shirts from before they could even make a move which was really very knowable of her. Mister Faulter had got very much fierce of the words made by the second brat's tongue that he wanted to pull his tongue and tie it up but he stayed calm instead and said bitterly "Don't even dare to look at my niece through your filthy eyes ! Leave our way !" "Oh ! She's your niece then we'd be needed to be much more affectionate as well as extra careful, right boys ?" Said the first men, his statement was being accepted by the others in a nodding manner.

Mister Faulter knew the drunkards very well, he knew that they would not let them go so simply and would keep speaking rubbish. After all what else drunkards would do – He thought.

He whispered to the triplets "Let us sprint before they could make a move." The four did as they'd plunged but haplessly only three of them were able to escape off their obstruction, the person who was ineffective, was the jet black-haired but that was because the drunkards had caught both of her arms firmly. "Evy !" Cried out uncle Jack and he along with the two boys ran towards her who was being held tightly by the drunk brats.

"DON'T DARE TO COME NEARER THAN IT OTHERWISE THESE BREATHS OF YOUR LOVELY NIECE WILL BE THE LAST ONES FOR SURE !" Yelled the second man in an alarming voice as he took off a very pointed skewer from his trousers' right pocket and placed it's sharp tip on the scared girl's neck by a side. This act had frightened the three individuals and all of them said together in a scared voice "Don't do anything to her !" As well as they stepped backwards as were being told to do so by the punk rascals.

"What had you thought we'll let you people go so easily ? No absolutely not, I knew that you wouldn't hand us this girl so simply but now you can see your very sweet niece is in our extremely secure clutch." Said the third man as he let out an evil laugh off his maw.

"So now we are taking this extremely beautiful lady with us and remember if you would make a single move towards us then you would lose her." Said the first man while smirking. "Kindly leave her, I'll give you whatever you want." Cried out mister Faulter as he was coerced to say so, Eveline could simply see the watery eyes of her uncle, scared as well as eyes full of rage of her best buddies and she could feel her eyes filled up with fright. "Well,

I would pay you instead if you let us take her without being troublesome to us." Said the second man who was still holding the girl tight enough to let her feel the misery. "Please be kind and leave her, I'm requesting you." Begged mister Faulter as he made his knees to touch the clean tiled-floor, on the contrast Jim and Sam were just resisting themselves from making any move towards the punk brats as if they'd do so then they would perhaps lose their friend as nothing could be said about the drunkards, either they could leave her or murder her but the position in which they were visioning their bestie had provided them with goosebumps all over their physiques.

"Hmm, sorry but we do not want to be, and yeah do not worry about this beauty, I assure you that we won't hurt her." Said the third man, "Well, we shouldn't waste our time, let us go guys." He said to the other two in his gang. They nodded and all of them said together to the three "Okay, we need to go now and do not dare to step forward otherwise you know what would happen; anyways see you later sweeties." "Uncle !" shrieked Eveline as her pretty eyes began to spill tears off them incessantly, "Don't worry darling, I said that we would not hurt you and I am hundred percent certain about it." Said the third man while smirking.

The brats began to move backwards while coercing the jet black-haired girl to do the same by forcing the tip of the skewer onto the edge of her neck hard enough to let a drop of pure red blood to trickle down her neck, their eyes were fixed on the three people whose eyes were on their partner. Uncle Jack was being compelled to stay still as he saw his niece in agony, Sam on the other hand intended to punch on the drunkards' faces but just like uncle Jack he was also being coerced to stay calm as he saw the blood trickle down his best friend's neck but Jim was profoundly thinking about something. The three were quietly watching the three men taking Eveline along with them as they saw them constantly moving backwards. It was such a shame to uncle Jack that in his presence some crooks were hurting his niece and he couldn't do anything in order to help her. The three men were just some meters away from the elevator but very far from mister Faulter, Jim and Sam in the sense of extrication as now if the three even wanted to save the jet black-haired girl then also they'd be unable to do so.

The men first made themselves to enter the lift but were needed to pull the girl so as to make her do the same then she set her feet into the elevator forcefully and the men along with the girl were whipped out of the three's sight as the hoist way door closed. Uncle Jack ran towards it following Sam and Jim.

He stood at the front of it all blank and dull, tears dripping down his cheeks whereas Sam stood stunned not able to manipulate and digest that a chunk of bad people took away Eveline, approximately ten minutes would have passed like this when Sam turned behind in order to say to his best friend that they should do something but was extremely stunned to view no one at his behind, he looked at his left, right even between his legs but was surprised to see nobody and cried out to uncle Jack "Mister Faulter ! They also took Jim along with them !"

Mister Faulter was stunned to hear that but when he gazed around he was also unable to view the handsome blue-haired boy and he admitted that the drunkards had caught him too. "What should we do now ?" Asked Sam hurriedly and worriedly "Let me call the cops." Said mister Faulter and took out his mobile phone and was just dialing when he heard a very familiar scream from his behind "Uncle Jack !"

He and Sam turned and were absolutely stunned as well as delighted to see Eveline bolting towards them from the staircase that wasn't too far away from them after her they could view a dark blue-haired boy strolling satisfyingly though he had some wounds on his physique but the way in which he was walking it didn't seem like they were mutilating him. As she reached close to them, she was being squeezed by her uncle's firm arms whereas Sam was awaited to hug her too and she did caress him too. After that she didn't say anything but only swiveled herself, hugged her very best friend and broke down completely and said to him while staying in the hug "Thank you so much Jim ! Thank you so-so-so much !" And she broke apart.

The two were delighted but baffled too & were awaited for an explanation; finally Jim said "Well, it was just that I'd heard a spell scrupulously." "Hey tell them with precision; okay let me tell." Said Eveline and after taking a deep breath and a pause she began "Well those filthy drunk men took me to the ground floor, after which they were pulling me on the deserted street, to come along with them to their home but then suddenly we all heard a voice from our behind and guess whose voice it'd have been ? It was certainly Jim's voice. The drunkards weren't pleased to see him though I was that was obvious. But they coerced him to move backwards by hurting me with the skewer and that was when they and I were stunned to see his heroic deed, the thing was he casted a spell due to which a red beam of light erupted off his right hand which was pointing towards the sharp ornament and it hit it, in return it vanished out of everybody's sight, the spell was 'Vanisho', after that I bit the man's hand who was holding me and ran up to Jim. But still we were needed to fight off the three men which seemed really difficult but then something struck Jim's sharp mind and he said to me to cast the spell with which he'd be able to survive the mutilations the men would provide him with, I was not certain that I would be able to do it or not but I did it and fortunately it did go all well. But all thanks goes to Jim that he fought the brats perfectly, while he was warring violently as well as bravely with them, not only I but those disgusting drunkards were also amazed to see his really good mixed martial arts and it was easily manifested by the way he was squabbling with them that he is an expert. After that, they sprinted out of sight and now we are standing in front of you."

Uncle Jack hugged Jim very rigidly that he scuffled but uncle Jack didn't let go of him until Sam had called out to him anxiously "Uncle, you'd clog him off !" Jim was relieved when he got liberated off the squeezing-squashing clasp of mister Faulter and breathed hardly on the very jiff he was released by him although uncle Jack felt embarrassed for being over compassionate and that is why he apologized to the dark blue-haired boy though he interrupted in the middle and assured him that it was all fine. Uncle Jack said as a grin appeared on his face "I am really very obliged that my Evy got such a tender buddy like you Jim and I know she's too." He expected his niece to nod though instead she spoke with pride in her voice "Of course I am."

Meanwhile Sam was unable to get it down his throat how come his bro managed to do that as he was just a novice and had not yet begun to study in the magical school then how did he do it.

Subsequently after letting out that agreement the jet black-haired girl had groaned due to which she got an instant notice of all the three persons, the gash on her neck was bleeding heavily and that was the cause of her groaning and moaning like that. The two boys bolted to examine the lesion but uncle Jack said quickly as he got a sight of his niece's groaning "We need to hurry up cause then only I can apply ointment on it." It seemed like his tediousness was dissipating from the very jiff he saw his niece being mutilated.

The four scampered forward to the room as Eveline's injury began to spill off more pure blood, her neck had drenched from it while she kept her groaning extremely down so as to prevent from getting anxious looks from her best friends who were seizing her sturdily in order to prevent her from getting stolen once again and this anxiousness of theirs had turned vigilant as well as adorable for the girl as their grip persistently tightened up.

As uncle Jack's strolling came to a cease, the others' movement also ceased. They stood in front of a wooden door, uncle Jack took out a keychain with a single key clinging to it off his pocket, he inserted it into the keyhole, out came a solid voice, he put it back into his pocket, turned the doorknob and the door swung open smoothly.

As the triplets' eyes curtailed they saw a tidily furnished hall – a room nicely adorned with three comfy sofas out of which one was bigger than the other two and it stood in the middle of both of them though all of them were across an easy wooden table on which a vase was resting in standing position with no flowers in it also a magazine was lying on the table, a television which was kept on a wooden stand that was fixed to the wall, a subtle wardrobe that was closed, stylish curtains were drawn on the only windows in the room, an umbrella holder with an umbrella in a corner of the entrance, a bookshelf with a few novels placed on the left side of the cupboard, some very uncanny paintings on the wall, an elementary wall clock and finally a door just beside the wardrobe which was certainly the way to the other rooms.

The triplets made themselves seated on the biggest couch but uncle Jack didn't sit instead he went to the only wardrobe in that room, unclosed it, took off a first aid box, without even bothering to close the cupboard he came up to his niece, sat beside her, kept the first aid box onto the wooden table, took out an antiseptic cream, a bandage and some cotton swabs. At first he wiped off the blood neatly from her neck from the cotton swabs while Eveline's friends felt bad that they could not help her as they saw her face expressions of extreme pain. After cleaning the blood, he took the ointment on one cotton ball and began dabbing onto her deep wound while she kept letting out low yells of agony, after applying the ointment adequately, the man picked up the bandage and put it on the healing gash. He grabbed the things and kept them back into the box and got onto his feet when Sam said to him "Jim is also wounded." He said while smiling weakly as he went to the wardrobe to put the box back onto It's respective place "Well, he won't need a first aid instead he'll need magic for his injuries."

This comment of the man substituted the triplets' facial expressions from their specific ones to nonplussed, they all looked at the man with sterling dubiety though the man just grinned at them weakly. He made himself to sit beside Jim as he made space for him to do that while stuttering to his buddy to shift a bit, after that he asked him "What do you mean by that ?" Uncle Jack gaped at him for some seconds then said in one go "The wounds aren't sore, are they ?" Jim answered rapidly "Yes you are right, they are actually not and in fact I don't even feel like I have been gashed. But-

but how ?" Mister Faulter gave an appealing grin though unenergetic and responded "That's cause of the incantation by which you've been bounded with and would continue to be bounded unless somebody casts an anti-charm." The three gazed at him then the dark blue-haired boy said "So it means when one would cast an anti-incantation on me then I'd feel all the agonies of these injuries which I've got ?" Mister Faulter nodded and continued to say "Well, the survival spell's meant for to survive in a maladaptive situation, not for to take away all the pains cause it's not made for it though they can be borrowed but can't be eliminated from one's lifespan." Sam asked curiously "Masarah casted that spell on us when we were about to come here but she didn't cast any anti-spell when we made it to this world, why so ?" Uncle Jack stood up and with his hands behind his back folded alike senior citizens, turning serious he explained "That's cause you children are neither aware nor habitual of this world's geographical conditions, therefore you're being in the necessity of making yourselves adaptive to it but the people who come here and are new, they'd be under the amidst of the survival incantation for a few years of their beginning I dunno how many but I know they're not plenty of them and the reason why I said that you'd need magic for your injuries is particularly that what I told you right away."

Sam turned a bit conscious for his bro and mumbled to himself as he shook his head down in despair "Does it mean he will be having those pains in a while ?" Uncle Jack would have heard him certainly that is why he did reply though without glancing "Yes certainly he'll be." Sam lifted his head to him and asked "It ain't important, is it ? I mean if it could be avoided to-to get those-" "Yes it does has much more importance than your envisaging."

Interrupted the man sharply as he got to understand what Sam was going to let off, Jim and Eveline didn't dare to speak anything just were hearing the serious discussion. Sam's voice changed from polite to cold as he said "But why couldn't we just postpone it to let Jim relax a bit coz he just fought off ? And I'm damn sure that you also know how much tedious it would've been for him." Uncle Jack's tone also turned cold "I do know that Sam, but we can't delay it cause we'd already done enough of it and hence couldn't help ourselves with more of it cause that'll be quite problematic for Jim as the torments would aggravate by time and would get fathomless and then it would be very much struggling for him to deal with the profound affliction and I bet you'd not want that to happen." Sam said nothing but his eyes said everything, his eyes did say that he could not believe on the stuff mister Faulter had said but then too he did not want his bro to suffer. And most probably for the sake of his bro he did end up responding as he'd got nothing to say else than that "I-I don't know what to say but I with absolute surety won't want Jim's afflictions to be intensified."

Uncle Jack looked at him with a low energetic grin then asked Jim with no smile rather earnestness "What bout you ? Are you ready for the anti-charm cause I'll be the one who'll cast it ?" Jim without any retardation said at once "Yes I am ready." Uncle Jack said with utter astonishment in his voice "Are you sure ? I mean I know there's no option as we can't delay it but then also aren't you horrified of the fact that very soon you'd be in unbearable or as I hope bearable pain cause I think or I might be wrong too but according to what I've learnt until now bout magic is that if somebody is being bounded by survival incantation then he or she is needed to be anti-charmed instantly after the purpose is done cause if he or she still is under it then his or her afflictions would exacerbate by time, hmm if I say precisely then in a total of sixty seconds it would increase by ten times." Sam and Eveline glanced at him incredibly after which they exchanged frightened looks but on the other hand the blue-haired boy remained tranquil while wondering how many minutes have been passed since Eveline casted the charm on him, when he got that uncle Jack was finished saying or should be said scaring him, he answered politely "Well, that's kinda obvious that it's terrific to think that soon I would be having unendurable agonies but if I'll keep my mind distracted which is the massive defiance as our mind only concentrates on the topic which is not listless and certainly gaining torments won't be a thing to leave unfocused but if we still think about it critically then we'd get to know that it is on the contrast a merit too as although our brain has quite many thoughts bopping into it at just a jiff but it can only pay whole of it's attention to one of it at a time, all the thought needs to get the mind's entire assiduousness is profundity and it couldn't be gained but the thought itself has to be sturdy enough. But I've got a thought which has perception, which would be suffice for me to be diverted." The two wondered which thought was enough to get all of his attention even when he would be going through with extreme amount of afflictions while uncle Jack whispered to himself "No thought would be able distract you."

Mister Faulter said to him "Okay then be ready and yeah let me clear it to both of you." He turned towards his friends then continued "That it might happen that he'd be yelling after I'd have anti-spelled him, and you might vision him thumping the floor, rolling on the floor, or even whacking his fists on the walls if the torments would be worst of worst but do not come to think of it that these afflictions will lead to his demise cause it never happens." Sam and Eveline gulped then nodded hesitantly while gazing at Jim who was beaming confidently, his eyes seemed to say to them 'Don't be anxious about me, I will be alright.' "Get ready Jim !" Said uncle Jack energetically, Jim nodded tranquilly. "Oivivrus !" Shouted out the man with whole of his power and out emcrged a dark black beam of light and struck Jim at his chest very swiftly like a bullet from a pistol does to its target.

For some jiffs Jim was not able process what just happened to him as he felt an intense wave of affliction emerging from the cavernous soul of him, from his insides a very deep and dreadful thunder of torments erupted, that storm did not just helter-skelter his serenity but also had deranged his insides. His physique was sweeping the tiled-flooring while his maw was yowling consistently, Sam and Eveline weren't able to whip off their eyeballs from him though they wanted to do so as they could not see their buddy shrieking & screeching like that and Jim had not done so before, he had never felt this much pain before, it was his first experience for certain. The two buddies wanted to help him but haplessly they could not do anything other than watching him yelling, the girl was feeling very guilty as she considered herself to be perpetrator for this ambience and for her friend's state of misery. Uncle Jack thought, to remain speechless would be a better option than conversing as he was the one who had hurled the incantation on the dark blue-haired boy whose condition was neither too worse nor too charming. Sam made a move towards his friend who was persistently curtailing on the ground with loud screams but uncle Jack pulled him back, Sam got fretted up and asked aloud "How much more he has to tolerate ? When would it be over ?" Mister Faulter said to him while making sure he was still in his sturdy clutch "I can't tell you that as I don't know myself but I can assure you that it would be over in a while but until that please maintain tranquility." Eveline said to him anxiously while glimpsing at her tormented friend "He'll be alright Sam, it is for his own good, be serene."

Jim was screaming so heavily that uncle Jack was needed to thrust his fingers into his ears but the two friends were just getting coerced to do the same although they did not do it as they could not keep their minds as well as eyes off Jim but when they noticed mister Faulter doing that, they felt it to be very much merciless of him as how could he behave like a stone-hearted person although uncle Jack did it just because of the deafening yowls of the boy.

The injuries on the boy's body began to fade away as his screeches got deafened and deepened, Sam and Eveline were delighted to see that though nonplussed that's why they both asked together "How it's happening ?" Uncle Jack who had not just shut his ears but also his eyes, unclosed them abruptly as he heard some words but did not get them, he stared at them as they did so as well then once again they asked the same question and fortunately he heard and responded solidly as Jim's screeches grew louder & louder "It happens when the agony is about to cease." Although the doublets had heard him barely but somehow they read his lips, got him and beamed contentedly. Eveline said to herself "Just a bit more Jim and then you will be emancipated off this nasty misery."

Just when the timepiece on the wall had struck half past ten the boy's yowling and howling began to slow down, the three people looked at him incessantly. Soon came a time when his yelling came to an end but he abided his mind who recommended him to continue to exist on the ground, his eyes remained closed, his heart throbbing speedily but the quietude he was getting was an absolute reward to him which he did deserve after the grimmest period, whether he was relishing it or easily having it, that could not be briefed as his expressions were a mixture of joy, tranquility, rage, horror and many more emotions. The three were gazing at him yearningly but he considered the position to be very much calming. Though he was aware that three anxious individuals were eyeing him persistently but it did not seem like it was bothering him.

Both of his friends were very awaited for their buddy to get all normal but the way he was lying on the floor seemed to make them anxious about him, they wondered whether he was okay or not but they kept quiet and still kept waiting.

After some more prolonged (for Jim's best friends) jiffs, the moment for which the three were waiting for so long came as Jim got up, all of his lesions were gone, he looked alright not like before when his face had contorted, Sam and Eveline asked him together delightedly "Still feeling any pain ?" Jim said quickly while beaming at them "Na, I'm feeling much better." Sam and Eveline were quite charmed up after listening those words that they ran to squeeze him by their awaited arms. Jim also ended up relishing it as he essentially as well as genuinely needed it after the stern agony. While the three were indulged in their amiable embrace uncle Jack slipped off the room through the door beside the cupboard. When the three broke apart after spending some jiffs being in one another's compassionate arms turned baffled as they made themselves aware that mister Faulter was not around them to watch them being engrossed in an affectionate caress.

"I think he has gone inside." Said Sam while pointing his index finger at the door beside the wardrobe, Eveline and Jim gave an act of agreement by nodding their respective heads. "So shouldn't we go too ?" Asked Sam urgently as he noticed their nods, Jim and Eveline looked at him with utter stupidity, Jim was not left to say anything as Eveline had already said quite enough to make him understand etiquettes "Are you insane ? You mean to say we can roam hither and tither in someone else's house without even bothering to ask him or her for his or her consent. Sam be mannered, you should know that it's not a good etiquette, at least think what would that person think about your personality, what impression you would have on him or her. I think I'm needed to make you reminded of the fact that you are a human being not an animal because animals do not think about manners as they don't have any shame but a respected human does think about them as he does has shame. And for your very kind information, you are tended to be a human being and you are unfortunately." Sam had hardly heard the ending words of hers intentionally as he knew perfectly that if Eveline would explain him something then she would certainly let some disrespectful words off her maw for him as she every so often intended to provoke.

# JIM'S APPALLING NIGHTMARE

Jim prevented Sam from being abased & also he did not want any quarrel to take place in between them not just as he was fed up of their contretemps but also because he was not in the state that he could endure any mental torture (the squabbles were certainly a sort of persecution to him) as his head was bursting not because of any agony as all of it had dwindled long ago but because of the words he'd heard the dark black-haired boy saying in the manager's office. Most probably for the sake of avoiding one more verbal fight, he ended up exchanging the topic with easiness of mister Faulter's house.

"Yes Jim it is indeed very well maintained, and I am quite surprised from his manageability as though he's living all alone with having no one to share his emotions but then also he has organized his home quite perfectly. I do want to appreciate him." Said Sam while glancing at the the sustained maintenance of the room. Jim was well pleased for the no longer perpetuated argument and said finely "Yeah and despite of being lonely he always manages to grin blazingly, at first I admitted him to be contemplative but now I do not think the same, though I still agree with the fact that he is a bit critical to get at sometimes but as long as I think of him, my considerations immediately change but one thing is very much clear that is he is very much concerned for us." While Jim and Sam were discussing about the girl's uncle, she was just hearing them scrupulously, at some jiffs she did feel infuriated by the ridiculous words the boys were letting off their mouths for her uncle but whenever she got to hear the eulogizing words she felt really good, in fact she also felt her face to be blazing at some moments furthermore she avoided being sighted by the two whenever she went scarlet all over her cheeks though she looked exquisite.

"Didn't keep you waiting for so long, did I ?" A voice came from nowhere else than off that door, Jim and Eveline looked at it expecting mister Faulter to emerge from its behind whereas Sam was baffled to hear as according to him it was peculiar, he gaped across the room and even he leapt to stare beneath every single article kept on the table, Eveline while gazing at him along with obvious silliness rubbed his forehead, she felt embarrassed by his deportment but Jim was feeling awkward, he wanted Sam to cease his ridiculous activities but Sam on the other hand continued giving scrutinizing looks to every location where he leaped to check in.

As Sam was going to examine underneath the table, out bounced a big (not very giant just more than regular size) mouse, Jim & Eveline let it stand on the table comfortably whereas Sam felt pride on himself but it waned as he saw mister Faulter closing the door, coming towards them with a tray in his hands which had three hamburgers along with three glasses filled up to the brims with orange juice. The sight of food demented him and forgetting all, he ran up to him took the tray off his hands immediately, rushed back to the table, placed the tray onto it, picked up one hamburger from one hand and juice from the other one and subsequently as well as urgently began to gobble up the hamburger as he gulped down the big sip of the juice contentedly. Eveline shook down her face in discomfiture while Jim thought 'He actually needs a tuition about manners.'

"I'm really sorry for this behavior of him, uncle." Apologized the only girl as uncle Jack looked at Sam unbelievably, as he heard her, he turned his face at her and said softly "Not you but I should apologize for not asking you people for any refreshments and do not come to think that I'm minding. No not at all in fact I'm just wondering for how many hours you three have not got a proper meal down your throats." As the dark blue-haired heard him, he also began to think about it while Eveline responded politely "That's really very sweet of you but we are not starving." Jim looked at her in amazement and he knew that Sam would also have reacted like him but he was busy with his gorging and guzzling. "Does not look like." Said uncle Jack as he looked at Sam who was devouring delightedly. Just then Eveline stomach rumbled a bit and uncle Jack jerked his face from Sam to his niece and said "And now your tum also agrees with my statement, see how it is growling in order to tell me that my words are correct. Eveline don't be ruthless to your tummy, I made these hamburgers today, have them and yeah I don't need any argument of yours, as I'd told you before do not be formal in front of me." Uncle Jack stepped backwards towards the door from which he had come with the food and while vanishing behind it he said as he poked his head out of the space made by him by unclosing the door a bit "I'll be back in sometime but when I come back I want this tray to be cleaned off."

"Sam behave yourself !" Said Eveline to him as she saw uncle Jack went out of sight, Sam ignored her and kept eating. Eveline was quite furious on him that after those words she went vexingly quiet that she just took her burger in her hands and began to praise it's deliciousness to Jim whereas Jim responded less while having his burger as he did want to make a fuss by avoiding Sam.

As Jim took his eyes off Eveline while stuffing the last morsel into his mouth (yes he did eat very swiftly but he did chew adequately), his eyes stuck onto the rodent, he noticed it to beam gleamingly, Jim had not seen a rat grin before in his life that is why he found it to be stunningly surprising but on the other hand cute as well. While the girl kept taking bites over bites of her hamburger, Jim got the chance to turn towards the mouse as Sam was still pretty engrossed in gulping his juice. Jim held his right hand towards the mouse softly though known of the fact that it could sink it's teeth but somehow by the wide grin the mouse had made him certain that it would masticate his hand. And seriously the rat did not champ it, to his sterling hope instead of having it as a morsel he hopped securely and made itself to stand onto his hand which was obviously a motion that manifested its certitude that the boy would not harm it. And it was also an act that made Jim ask to himself whether the mouse felt secure in his hand otherwise it would not have made such a stunning move. Jim asked though knowingly that it would not respond "Who are you ?" But the next move the rat made, pushed Jim into quite a lot bewilderment as the rodent did answer "I am Gilberd." Coercing his larynx to let the shackled voice off the chains of bemusement, the boy said slowly "You-you can speak ?" The mouse noticed his perplexed face and replied "Yes I can talk like you humans and I am already being tamed by mister Faulter, yes I am his pet." The rat finished, Jim said "How come you can speak ?" This question for a jiff had discombobulated the rodent but after realizing what the boy was asking, he responded politely "I might not tell you everything because it would be divulgence but I can tell you that I am under the communication charm." Jim glanced at the rat and wondered whether an incantation could make the quadrupeds converse like human beings. "Yes it might be astounding for you but it is kind of ordinary thing that every person does to his pet when he comes to know of the existence of such a spell. By the way what is your good name ?" Asked the mouse tranquilly, Jim who had muted himself for sometime, responded quickly as he heard the rat "Oh, my name's Jim Sueruds. Nice to meet you." The rat beamed and said "Nice to meet you too mister Sueruds." Jim felt really good to hear that as no one had ever preferred to refer to him like that.

"So you met my pet." Called out a familiar voice, as he turned in its direction, he saw uncle Jack looking at him with a little smile on his face, Sam and Eveline who had nearly finished their hamburgers also looked at them. "Yeah and I liked him." Answered Jim as his friends came towards him while masticating the last bites and glanced at the rat that stood comfortably on his right hand. "Master, I liked him too." Said the rat which made the two children (who were unknown that it could communicate) bounce up. "Is this true or am I dreaming ? This rodent is-is talking like us !" Said the grey-haired boy getting bemused, Eveline also said getting confounded "This-this rat is-is-is-" "Talking, because I can do that." Completed the rat, Eveline and Sam remained baffled until the rat had let off his little mouth the same reason he had told Jim. Uncle Jack remained silent for the entire duration the two were talking to the rat whereas Jim was sticking with the thought whether he should have a pet in the future or not.

The three's conversation kept going on, now they were talking about how Gilberd found Jack Faulter. Uncle Jack found the discussion to be unvaried as Gilberd had already narrated the tale to dozens of people including his neighbors that is why he said to Jim as slowly as he could "Finding it dull ? I'm also in, so let us go for a walk." Jim looked at him astoundingly, the clock was striking five minutes to eleven, this time was of course not the right time to go out in the dark just because of getting fed up of a listless chat. And Jim did not want to move his legs as his left vigor had also drained off while wrestling with the punk rascals that is why he responded carefully as he also did not intended to upset the man while he heard the rat saying "I was at first very much arrogant and also was an introvert but master made me like what I am now, he made to open up, he told me that talking is not a big deal." "I am extremely sorry but I think I won't be able to accompany you with it as I'm not in such state, I mean I am no longer vital, you know coz of this tedious day I had along with them." Uncle Jack looked at him then he got what he understood and said urgently "Oh I didn't mean what you got, I meant if you'd like to have a look at my home." Jim said after some jiffs "Oh, is that what you were saying ? Then it is all fine. I will do it surely." Uncle Jack was happy that he agreed, he turned his head towards the three who were prettily involved in their gossip while letting out hearty laughs. "Wound you two like to join ?" He asked but as he had expected, they had not paid a bit of attention to him as they were busy with their chit-chats. "Well, I'll take it as a 'No', anyways Jim let us go." Jim nodded obediently.

The dark-blue haired followed mister Faulter, the man closed the door as Jim had made himself to enter into a bedroom which had three comforting beds despite of having one, he looked around; he saw that the room's walls were adorned with nice checkered designed wallpapers, three bedside tables were placed by a side by every bed on their lefts, on the drawers there were three little regular lamps, a sizeable cabinet stood in the very right corner that was closed, a door at the very left corner and a door at the very right corner just beside the cabinet. Uncle Jack said "This is your room." Jim looked at him all nonplussed "Yes this room will from now on belong to the three of you – You , Sam and my Evy and yeah that is the lavatory plus bathroom." Said mister Faulter as he pointed his hand at the door beside the cabinet, Jim was about to argue when uncle Jack said "Don't start it again. You know very well that I'd not listen a single argument of yours." Jim shook his head then said after a while "Shall we go to the next room then ?" Uncle Jack looked at him and asked "Won't you want to know how I arranged this room for you three ?" Jim who was smart enough to guess that it was the guestroom did not get bothered up when uncle Jack told the same.

The next room they visited was mister Faulter's bedroom, quite simple, adorned with the same designed wallpapers; a drawer just beside the bed with a lamp, an empty glass, a jug half-filled with water and a newspaper; a medium sized wardrobe closed for certain; a study table made of polished wood kept at the right corner with a table lamp, some files kept one over another which seemed to be hefty, an easy pen stand with many fountain pens, a stack of blank sheets, a sheet which lied with some writings on it, it looked as though the words were needed to be completed as a pen was lying aside the last word; a simple polished wooden chair that was kept close to the study table; a wooden polished door at the left and a simple plain door at the right.

"This is my room." Said mister Faulter as the dark-blue haired boy's eyeballs curtailed, Jim said to him "Mister Faulter, I must appreciate your manageability and maintenance. I know living in this killing loneliness is not uncomplicated, without having anybody to confess your sentiments it's quite challenging." Uncle Jack looked at him "You're talking like Evy. But it's not that much difficult though sometimes I do feel that, my family should've been with me but I can just envisage it. But now I'm finding it facile." Jim said as mister Faulter finished saying. "That's because you've been living here from numerous years. But then too it must be challenging." Uncle said while patting at the boy's shoulder "I'm not the only individual suffering, there're millions of people across the globe whose situations are also like mine." Jim said urgently as uncle Jack finished "Yeah that is indeed true but most of the people are agonizing in their isolation, they aren't able to manage a beam and to the top of all many have given up from being spruce, they have heaved up their hands in the case of orderliness and cleanliness." Mister Faulter blushed then again patted at Jim's broad shoulders "Jim, you're making me feel very special, anyways wanna see the kitchen ?" Jim nodded although he did not want to as his fatigued physique was not supporting his brain.

They made it to it via the door on the right. It was kind of simple but exceptionally tidy, porcelain- colored walls, a small pantry just beside an ordinary refrigerator that was kept in front of the kitchen sink at right side though leaving suffice space to stand (the back of the fridge was adjacent to the wall, it's unclosing in the contrasting direction of its back), some medium-sized base cabinets as well as wall cabinets of the same color – gray, a broiler oven kept at a suffice distance from the basin, a little sapling beside the oven, an easy but clean stove on the other side of the plant, a toaster kept just beside the stove on its other side, a neat stoned-floor, a regular dustbin kept at a corner alongside the refrigerator adjacent to the wall and a door that was on the left side which was the way to the dining room as the man told the boy scrupulously.

Next they set their feet into was the repository which was a bit mucky, large cartons which were shut by the tape attached at some openings, a sooty ladder whose one foot needed mending and a besom which struck the boy's eyeballs. "Oh ! A besom !" Uncle Jack responded "Yes it's my Lily's grandmother's, after her grandma's demise she used to use it, sometimes I also helped her out with the sweeping, I used to try to snatch it off her hands due to which we used to see one another stumbling on the dusty floor & then we chortled heartily; hmm I miss my family so much. Anyways Jim let's get out of here, your friends might be waiting for us." He let out a small tear off his left eye while hiding it from Jim's sight though he noticed it and said to him sympathetically "I'm very well aware, how it feels like when your loved ones leave you." Mister Faulter looked at his sorrowed expressions and then said "I don't want to hurt you but you can tell me how your parents demised, only if you want to." Jim shook down his head and said "They haven't demised, they're still alive." Uncle Jack looked at him astonishingly and said in a baffled voice "What ?! But you used to live in the orphanage, if your parents are still alive then how come you're not with them ? How come you ended up being in that orphanage ?" Jim's physique was shaking as he responded at once "That's coz they sold me." Mister Faulter was taken aback by his words, Jim's words had not just invited dead silence to end up to exist there for some difficult minutes but also those words of him had also brought gentleness in uncle Jack's heart for him.

Finally the man broke the silence "But-but why ?" Jim shook up his head and replied with rage in his voice "My dad was a drunkard, my mom was a housewife. At first my father did not drink at all but when he got a job, it made him distressed that he began to drink, not much in the beginning but later he got addicted to it, when mom advised him to cease it, he started to maul her hard enough for her to shut his mouth in the case of giving him her guidance or suggestions. The drinking not only adversely affected his health but also left a big impact on our financial condition as his addiction had got much exacerbated in an year that he began to blow his salary on the bottles, at that time I was an year old. Mother kept stopping him from doing so but he didn't listen to her, when all of his finances were blown off on his alcoholic misdeeds, he demanded for money from mother but she did not gave him a single penny as expected, in return she got mutilated severely that she left the man and the home without even bothering about me for once." Uncle Jack gasped astoundingly as he was about to ask something to Jim replied immediately "I know what you must be thinking, didn't anyone of our neighbors get to know about that filthy man's deeds, so I'd say yes the neighbors did know that my dad drunk." Jim sighed with rage then continued "But they did not get to know about the departure of the lady who had given birth to an unfortunate boy as that man whose blood is running in that boy's veins had coerced him to move along with himself to countryside where it was all deserted, no one ever got to know where the two fled away. After these many sins he did not change, he kept going on with his drinking but needed money in order to do that. Rather than earning he got any idea struck in his filthy mind which made him to-to sell the boy, he sold the boy christened as 'Jim' to a local man and obviously got money in return. After that, that boy never saw that man who belonged to him as a father." Uncle Jack looked at him with his watery eyes and patted at his back then Jim continued again "Somehow that boy extricated by fleeing away from the local man who had taken him to a big abandoned villa where many children were trapped though they were quite elder than him whereas he was just an year old. For two days the boy kept strolling without a single morsel or drop of water down his throat and obviously it had made him very much lean and weak. On the third day his eyes spotted an orphanage after which he made it to it and remained there until yesterday midnight. Sam was the first one whom he'd met around his third birthday." Jim had finished narrating his sad tale, uncle Jack gaped at his eyes in order to get whether he was crying or not but he got it very soon that he was not though his eyes were filled with immense infuriation for both of his parents.

"Overall he never got the opportunity to get the love of his parents, whenever he used to see some kids chilling with their mom and dad, he used to ponder why him, whenever someone asks him how his childhood is going on he does not reply at all as what is he supposed to say when he never got to know what childhood is. Eveline and Sam had at least spent some special moments with their mother and father, at least they got loved by them no matter what. But on the contrast is that boy who's this much hapless that does not even know what motherhood & fatherhood is in actual and that hapless boy in no one else than the boy who's standing in front of you." Finished Jim with disappointment in his eyes, his wordings were quietly raged. The man said to him as he saw no other words to come off his mouth "Jim I'm really sorry that I made you remind this trauma-" "You shouldn't be as this ain't a trauma instead I consider it to be a bliss coz it makes me feel special and different from other children." Intruded Jim with a fake beam. Uncle Jack did not say anything else just gazed at his face incessantly. Uncle Jack thought how much blissful he should be as he at least spent a total of thirty-nine years with his family but on the contrast was Jim who was not even aware of what does it actually mean by a family, He was lost in his profound thoughts when Jim broke his deepening thinking "Shall we leave then ?" Uncle Jack nodded hesitantly and they both got off the grimy repository.

When the two made it back to the living room they saw the three still gossiping and chuckling, when they made themselves to sit beside them on the couch, they were astounded that the three did took no notice of their presence well that was kind of patent when they did not sight their absence; now they were chatting about one another's favorite pastimes. Jim was very well aware of his friends', Sam's was sketching & painting whereas Eveline's was reading. "Mine is cheese." Told the rat when being asked, Sam asked "You meant having cheese, right ?" Gilberd nodded hastily then asked "What is Jim's ?" Both Sam and Eveline began to speak one after another "Experimenting" "Constructing gizmos" "Honing his martial skills" "Reading" "And devoting time to nature." Mister Faulter was stunned to see the doublets' credence though Jim was not flabbergasted by the fact that his buddies knew him flawlessly as this was not an unapparent thing to be critically thought, the three had been with one another from past many years and hence had got to know quite a lot about each othcr. "What's mister Faulter's ?" Asked Sam curiously to the rat and was also expecting it to answer but Eveline spoke before it could "He is a cuisine connoisseur." Sam said as quickly as he could "Oh, well I loved the hamburgers, they were like being prepared by a chef." Eveline beamed and said "Yes, he has an unending affection for cooking cuisines from a very long time." On the other hand mister Faulter could not hide his blushes, and it went wild when Jim commented "Yes mister Faulter I was also amazed by your culinary skills when I had mine burger into my buccal cavity." This statement made the three to jump from their positions a bit because of bafflement. Pushing his shyness aside, the man mustered up his voice from deep inside his throat and said "It seems as If I won't instruct you to be off for beds then you'd never leave your places and would continue your chit-chatting; have a look at the wall clock." The timepiece had struck half past eleven. Mister Faulter told the two unknown persons that the way to their room was not complicated, they were just needed to unclose the door to one side of the wardrobe in there. Then he told Gilberd to off for his burrow too. As the rat gilded off the table, made a soft landing on the tiled floor then strolled on his two short less furry legs towards his hole. After Gilberd's departure the triplets also rushed to lay on their beds as they were immensely exhausted by the terrible (in some ways) day.

Sam and Eveline did not lay down but instead they began taking looks of their room whereas the dark blue-haired boy whose eyes had already absorbed plumbed pictures of it had emerged out of nowhere other than their backs and had plopped on his cozy bed. After some jiffs discovering nothing peculiar and after leaving nothing unviewed, the doublets also went docile to their physiques as they reclined themselves on their respective beds. The triplets were left with no more vitality that is why they fall asleep as they changed their sides for a few times.

"Oh Lord Devil ! Lord Devil ! Please appear ! Please appear ! Your disciple needs you ! Lord Devil kindly appear !" A figure of a very young looking girl whose age would not have been more than twenty-five; who was in a pure black garments; who was tremendously fetching & who was unremittingly repeating those lines. For about incessantly saying those wordings for not more than three hundred seconds the girl's statements came to a cease as she charmingly sighted queer onyx colored cloudy hazes to erupt in the central area of the very dark and gloomy room where the girl stood enthusiastically awaited for something.

The murk took the form of an anomalous dark figure (how it actually appeared that could not be seen because of its intense darkness) which could not be briefed. "What do you want my child ?" Asked the figure in a bone-chilling tone though the sound was wholly profound "My Lord ! You are very much aware how I ended up being here, though I can very easily get out of this ruddy place but the thing which bothers me a lot is you are aware of." Answered the girl hastily without any delay. The figure took a pause then said "I am certainly aware what you are talking but that is not a thing to be anxious about. If you are anxious about being mor-" "I am patently not brooding about it as I do not need to be that in order to-" "DO NOT DARE TO INTRUDE WHEN I AM SPEAKING !" Yowled the figure as the girl had attempted to made an interruption, the girl fell silent in order to obey the figure not because she was horrified "So as I was saying that if you are anxious about it then there is no necessity for so because you are a particle of mine and therefore possess some of my miraculous powers as well which will assuredly assist you." Finished the figure heftily.

"My Lord I am not afraid of death, my heart is sterling and is devoted to you, if I have thc assistance of the darkest evil of this universe then why am I supposed to be scared and what am I supposed to be scared of, I just have a single wish of terrorizing the magical world with my dark skills, I want this world under my foot, I want gaiety to be evanesced off this world. At all I want to rule on this world once again. But how am I supposed to do that ? My condition is not so, kindly guide me my lord." Said the girl politely pronouncing every word scrupulously. "Wait, all you must do is to wait until someone foolish enters into this place after which he or she will make your aisle all cleared up, then you will be needed to get yourself adorned with a body, it will not matter by its physical appearance but the thing which will matter for certain is the person's mind, it will be needed to be evil just like you, it will be needed to be wicked, it will be needed to be sinful, it will be needed to be vile and to the top ot all it will be needed to be brilliant. After you would have got someone enthralled then all you will need is utilizing my powers." Finished the figure after which they took a pause and began to laugh evilly.

Then suddenly the figure began to warn in an alarming voice "But be aware of that person who will be a massive hindrance in your expedition because that person can also lead to your ultimate death." The girl said rapidly after the figure had finished letting off words in its hefty tone "Who will be that, lord devil ? In whose possession is that much enormous power that he or she can conquer over me. I had trounced that old dull-witted Rason and if I am not incorrect then he is the most influential warlock ever in this whole world after me, then who's there who can rout such a puissant witch like me ?" The figure answered tranquilly "At first you should not be conceited about being possessing immense powers or position and secondly you should not underestimate your foe although you had vanquished Rason but you should not forget that he was being mutilated by your disciples and then too being agonizing he was resilient and had given you a durable fight." The girl frowned but kept waiting for the figure to carry on but it did not carry on, then the girl said "I will certainly keep your words in my mind, my lord. But do you not know that person who will be an obstruction to me ?" The figure responded serenely "I do know but cannot tell you as it is an averse to my fundamentals." The girl asked impatiently "Then how would I identify that person if I ever meet him or her ?" The figure responded in his as usual frightening voice "You would get to know that as soon as that individual will be in your vicinity." The girl asked immediately "But how my lord as I have not been known to that person ? On the contrast it patently would consume immense time of mine to comprehend him or her and you are saying that I will get to know that as he or she would set his feet into my vicinity, but how am I supposed to get when he or she would be into it ?"

The figure replied with a bit of vexation in his voice though overall it sounded quite tranquil "I told you, you will get to know that as soon as that person sets his feet into your vicinity and now if you are anticipating me to go inimical to my principles then you are unquestionably erroneous." The girl was about to say but kept quiet as she saw the figure to continue "Once again I am making you cognizant of this very significant thing that do not ever underestimate your rival because you do not know who that person would be; no one knows who it could be, so do not consider that he or she could not be an under aged individual. But also do not come to think of it that you do not possess sufficient power to conquer over him or her because you do have it as you had vanquished Rason." The girl responded "Yes, I will not disappoint you my lord. Thank you for bestowing your precious time to this insignificant disciple of yours." The figure did not respond but disappeared out of sight, after which the girl began to laugh hauntingly.

Jim roused up joltingly, his entire physique was damped with the perspiration that had occurred due to the recent ephialte and his hidrosis was patent as the terror filled scenes he had just envisaged unknowingly nowhere else than in his own clever brain were implausible. Along with sudorific the nightmare was undeniably far-fetched as well. Jim was sitting on his no longer cozy bed as it had been drenched thoroughly by his own cold sudor. After a while he came back to his sensible senses and wondered horrifyingly about whatever he had seen.

What had he seen actually ?! Was all of it true or was it just a frivolously terrific dream of him ? Who was that girl ? Had she invocated the devil for real ?! But why had he dreamt this all ? As he'd never been dreaming about such terrible things although he had also had many nightmares in his past. These questioning thoughts were lingering in the dark blue-haired boy's sharp mind as he glanced at the drop of sweat which had fallen on his palm's back from his nose. On the other hand his friends were sleeping cozily also they seemed like beaming, on their specific beds. The boy seized his wristwatch that he'd kept on the side table before getting deep in his sleep and gaped at what time it was. It was 3 o'clock at midnight, he placed it back onto it and got off his bed. He had no thought of disrupting his friends' saccharine dreams just because of his own contrasting one. After shuffling his feet for about an hour finally he got tedious and got back to his bed.

The same boy livened up because of hearing noises of some arguments, he at his full tilt darted towards the direction from where the noises were coming and in a trice he got to know that the noises were being discharged off his friends' quarreling mouths.

"What happened ?" Asked Jim to the two who were sitting side by side on the dining table while mister Faulter was sitting in their front. The two swiveled their heads to notice Jim to emerge out from their back who was closing the door from his right hand and was rubbing his left eye with another hand. He took the seat beside Sam who had saved it for him by insisting uncle Jack to take another seat. As Sam sighted Jim to cease his rubbing, he immediately told him "Jim now you're the only one left who can explain to her that I am not a kid anymore, I do possess some self respect, do I not ? But she often treats me as I'm reckless, I don't know anything. At first she complains to me when I don't make her aware of some ridiculous stuff (according to her) then she is the one who brawls with me for the entire duration if she finds the thing to be peculiar which every so often happens, right ?"

Jim who was neither pathetic nor flummoxed as he was jaded of his friends' frequent contretemps and also he wasn't unknown to it that once again his friends would have been debating about a nasty topic or once again Eveline would've been a pedagogue to Sam for any of his fault, Jim who had no concern to get himself into their argument asked "If you'll tell me what has happened then I might be able to provide a solution." Before the two can speak mister Faulter said to Jim "I don't know how you tackle with their perennial rows, you know they've been quarreling since the moment they've set their feet here, I guess an hour has elapsed but they're consistently arguing." The two fell silent. Then Mister Faulter asked Jim if he had freshened up to which he responded back that he was left with it and told the three over there that he would be back within some jiffs. And the boy sprinted towards the bathroom.

After sometime Jim came back fully invigorated although his eyes still seemed bit sluggish, it was like he had not had a good sleep. He sat beside his friends and began to devour on his toast with milk kept in his dish prettily along with three boiled eggs, an apple, two sausages, fried mushrooms and an uncanny little food item wrapped in black aluminum foil; as it struck Jim's eyes Sam without any delay said "That's a traditional chocolate of MMW which is made by the local people when an official person dies, although it looks kinda unusual but it is actually very delicious." Jim asked after swallowing the large bite of toast stuck in his throat "But who has died ?" Eveline answered as she saw Sam busy with his last boiled egg "The chieftain of mumbo-jumbo tribe." Jim looked at her then asked while picking up a fried mushroom "Tribe ? Are there tribes out here somewhere ?" Eveline replied after taking a sip of milk from her glass "Uncle says there are, in the densest greenwoods of this world of occults, right uncle ?" Mister Faulter nodded instead of replying back as he always did though he wanted to respond but his mouth was full of soggy sausages.

At nearly half past eight the four were done with their breakfast, the boys were about to begin their race towards their room when they heard Eveline asking her uncle "I'll help you out uncle." To this statement of hers, her uncle beamed at her the patted on her head and said to her passionately "No need Evy, until now I've done everything all by myself and am not in the habit of getting assited." But Eveline argued "But not anymore, now I'm here and I won't let you do everything all by yourself, I'll help you and as you say to me every so often 'I'd not listen a single word of yours in it.' So I'm also saying the same, I won't listen any word of yours, I'll assist you and that's final." Uncle Jack was about to let another argument off his maw when his niece rushed towards the kitchen, he was certain what his niece would do next.

As the three followed her darting, they saw her doing the wishes, Jim and Sam felt ashamed of themselves and hurriedly said to uncle Jack altogether "We'll also help you, just tell us what should we do ?" Mister Faulter responded immediately as he heard them "I'd not let you do anything for me, you're my-" "We aren't your guests but are your nephews like Eveline and you said it yourself, remember ?" Interrupted Jim politely, mister Faulter looked at him, grinned then said "Yeah you are undoubtedly but I'd not want my nephews to work for-" "Your niece is that then why can't we ?" Intruded Sam keeping in mind to be polite.

Mister Faulter was left with no option than assigning them a few works, he kept in mind to provide them with facile jobs as he said to them "Hmm, fine I got it I can't get triumph against you children. I'll be obliged if you'll do the dusting of all the cupboards while I'll do the mopping."

"I'll do it." Said out a soft voice, the three swiveled and saw Eveline standing in front of them whose dress had not turned saturated but was a bit dampened up, uncle Jack said to her "No Evy I'll do it." Eveline argued "No uncle I can do it." Jim and Sam said together "We'll do it !" The two looked at them then asked together "Do you people even know how to do it ?" Jim answered politely "Eve don't you remember we both used to do it for the caretaker ?" He pointed his index finger towards him and his friend – Sam while saying. Eveline gaped then replied "Oh yeah I remember that, hmm then you two can do it and I'll do the dusting." The three headed off to do their respective jobs before mister Faulter could say anything else. He laughed to himself as all of them disappeared out of sight then said to himself "I bet their parents would be extremely indebted to have such kids. They remind me of Alex." He let out a tear from his right eye.

The children were engrossed in the works been assigned to them, Jim and Sam were busy with the sweeping and mopping while Eveline was indulged in dusting but uncle Jack was making preparations of their lunch although it was only nine, when the triplets' tasks were over they went in the look of mister Faulter and were not stupefied to spot him preparing the lunch as he'd be off for his job in a while and would arrive back in the dusk.

When the time was not far from ten, mister Faulter was getting ready to be off for his errand whereas the triplets were in their room: Sam had asked to mister Faulter if he could borrow a sheet to which he obviously said beamingly "You don't need to ask me." As Sam heard him, he took an art sheet from mister Faulter's room and went up to his room and began sketching; Jim's face was buried in the academic Science book and Eveline was trying out her school robes (patently not in the front of the boys but in the dressing room that was attached to the bathroom) and was customarily questioning to her friends how she was looking, Jim and Sam had nothing other than to appreciate her beauty as she looked exquisite.

At quarter past ten mister Faulter emerged in their room and instructed them to lock the door from inside as he was going. The jet black-haired girl strolled behind her uncle and as being told she obediently locked the door, returned back to the room and carried on with her work.

# CHAPTER NINE

# OLASKOVOCIK MANTONIOUS SCHOOL OF MAGIC

Days passed by and it did not take any long for the last day of their stay in mister Faulter's home to arrive, the sky turned from azure to cerise, soon the sun set and it turned from cerise to dusk; the triplets' enthusiasm was reaching the zenith which was simply manifested by their faces but uncle Jack on the other hand was dismal as he would no longer be able to see the three children in his house as the three would be needed to leave tomorrow and would live in the boarding school (OMSOM had a hostel attached to it). Uncle Jack had associated himself with the three intuitive children that is why at night he ended breaking entirely into the three's arms, allowing large tears to stream down his damp cheeks, allowing the three to know about the boarding school, allowing his sturdy solicitude to emanate out from his chest, allowing his niece to become a bit emotional too and finally requesting the boys to take care of his niece; he was off to bed after dictating them to finish off their packing.

"Aren't you done yet ?" Asked Jim to Sam whose face was still buried in his suitcase "Just a bit left." Responded he without looking at him. Eveline was lying on her bed, reading a book very scrupulously that was handed by her uncle to her whereas Jim was easily watching Sam.

It seemed like the nightmare had dwindled away from his clever brain otherwise he would have told his friends about it and would have also argued with Eveline about it, being a nightmare.

It was seven in the morning of the first of May, the triplets were deep in their sleep when mister Faulter came in and woke them up. They got up being invigorated though a bit sleepy "Get ready ! We've to depart at quarter to eight." He said cheerfully while leaving the room. The three took baths as fast as they could, finished scrubbing their teeth, and were totally prepared when mister Faulter came to call them for the breakfast.

"I am very happy !" Said Eveline as she picked up a mug of coffee out of the four kept on the dining table, "That's kinda obvious as you're an incorrigible bookworm." Commented Sam as he took a bite of the bread with a large amount of butter on it. Eveline did not understand whether her friend had passed a positive or a negative comment for her that is why she stayed quiet which Sam considered as ignorance due to which he did not say anything else to her after that comment.

"Now go and fetch your suitcases ! We are all set to go !" Announced the forty-years old man over there. The three went to their room, seized their hefty suitcases & came back while gasping.

The four set about onto their feet to be off the apartment, stood on the busy street; when the triplets asked mister Faulter how they were supposed to reach the school, he responded back to them "I've booked a taxi for the four of us, it'd be here in a moment; though the school is not much far but it would almost take half an hour for us to be there."

It took no longer for the four to be in an ordinary car which was moving incessantly but smoothly with no pause at all. Uncle Jack was comfortably conversing to the taxi driver whether the taxi was his own or someone else's and what was the price of it, Jim was listening the conversation scrupulously whereas Sam and Eveline were engaged in admiring the alluring sites which came into the reach of their eyeballs.

"What's that ?" Asked Sam with his index finger held out at a shabby tall tower surrounded by electrical fences all over it on a very vast wall around it. "That's Nordes." Replied the driver before uncle Jack could, mister Faulter glared at the driver although he did not notice it. "What ?" Asked Jim bafflingly, "It's the biggest prison of our world." Responded the driver once again before uncle Jack could speak. "I have not thought this world would need a jail." Said Sam turning his face towards Jim from the window, "Well it does need because not all of the people can be virtuous, right ?" Asked mister Faulter before the driver could, the three nodded sincerely, "There're many dreadful wizards as well as witches whom this world is terrified of and it is very much important for the three of you to be with each other every so often as you don't know what is waiting for you in the future." Said uncle Jack in a cautioning tone. Jim asked "Are you aware of any witch or wizard ?" Uncle Jack gaped at him then answered "Yes indeed I am. Many long years ago, a witch had unfolded the clandestine aisle to make it to the darkest evil of rectitude, the witch was to be called as 'Sarah Bones' who was extremely renowned for being the proprietor of black magic and the only person to be brilliant at necromancy." Sam asked bemusedly "Necro-what ?" Uncle replied "Necromancy" Sam asked again "What's it ?"

Uncle Jack responded seriously as the children's heads had swiveled towards him and they were awaited to hear what it was, "It is the art of dark magic which involves communication with the dead by summoning their spirits as visions or apparitions in order to do divination or for other purposes." Eveline had her hands on her maw, Sam was astounded whereas Jim had no reaction but was simply looking at uncle Jack. "Does she still exist ?" Asked Sam curiously, uncle Jack was about to respond when the taxi driver said "No she was killed."

The car took a sharp turn which had caused the four to leap, that was when Jim asked quickly "Killed ? By whom ?" "She was defeated as well as killed by OMSOM's very much strong, tough, powerful, alert and very smart superintendent." Replied uncle Jack. "You used many appreciative wordings for him, does he actually deserve them ?" Asked Sam ridiculously, Eveline elbowed him. "Don't you ever dare to say anything rubbish about him !" Said the taxi driver bitterly while handling a fierce look to the grey-haired boy via the inner rear-view mirror. Uncle Jack was about to say something when Eveline said politely "He's very foolish, by the way who's that brilliant person ?" "Sir Ra-Oh we've arrived." Said the taxi driver as the journey took a cease. The three got off the taxi whereas uncle Jack remained in the car as he had to make it back to his house, he wished them "All the best ! Do study well. And do not miss me Evy. I'll meet you in your winter vacations, goodbye !" The taxi turned and departed off with mister Faulter waving his hand to the three.

The three stood in front of a giant gate which was closed; numerous children dressed the same like the triplets and also had big suitcases, were gossiping with each other, many of them looked quite younger while many were much elder than the three whereas some looked as the same as the three in terms of age group. The three spotted Masarah standing in the front of the children, robed in white, it looked as though she was about to give a speech. The triplets did their best to stand in the front so as to converse with her & tell her about what had happened with them until then but haplessly had to do with the second position.

"A very warm welcome to all of you ! For the new ones I just want to say – Don't be nervous, you'll do great and will enjoy a lot and for the old ones – I hope you enjoyed your vacations and are totally prepared to dive back into your studies but do not forget that fun won't stop. So WELCOME TO OLASKOVOCIK MANTONIOUS SCHOOL OF MAGIC !" Yelled Masarah charmingly with a wide grin on her wrinkled face, she continued "The old students, I don't think I'm in the necessity of making you aware of the pathway." Masarah waved both of her hands in a peculiar manner which ended up unclosing the massive gate, most of the students went inside as the gate fell unclose.

After it, Masarah said "And new students before entering in, you're needed to have one of these." The caretaker pointed her wrinkled hand towards a sizeable polished squared metallic container which was opened, when the left students peered into it they saw many rectangular plate-like structures with a screen on a side, they were 6 centimetres wide and 10 centimetres long. Each student picked one of those one by one and glanced at them bemusedly like they hadn't seen a thing like it before in their lives, and when the triplets' turn came, they weren't bewildered to get them into their hands as they were familiar to them. They were cell phones – the electronic devices which every person in their dimension had.

"This is a mobile phone." Jim said though not very loudly but he had got everybody's eyes on him. A very hesitant looking boy said slowly "Yes he is right, I've seen it in daddy's hands many times." The three looked at the boy who looked away nervously. "Yes students these're mobile phones but in MMW we refer to them as 'Celluthin Pheckum'. Our very honorable principal had launched a rule the previous year that every student will have his own celluthin pheckum. It has many wonderful features like-" "Easy, fast and secure communication; convenient tools for learning; easy access to information; internet browsing; multitasking power; amazing entertainment sources and easy navigation facilities." Interrupted the dark blue-haired boy, the old lady glanced at him beamingly, every student gazed at him with bewilderment as they wondered 'Who's this boy who knows this much about a gadget that we had never seen before ?' "Very good, so as he said, these are certainly the features of them but do remember it that our honorable principal has provided it to you just because of your own safety, convenience and in order to make your lives a bit easier than before, like if you miss any lecture and possess a query then, instead of disturbing your friends you can simply ask about it to the subject teacher. A particular data will be provided to you every month and it'll be entirely your responsibility to use it wisely according to your needs as if you'll blow it on entertainment then you might regret later when you'll actually need it." Said Masarah seriously while smiling widely.

"Now come after me everybody !" Said she energetically and loudly for everyone to hear her. The students began to follow her.

As the long queue entered the gateway they had to curtail their eyeballs in order to cherish the vast view of the huge playground, in their front was a very expansive as well as very lofty edifice with countless floors although the entire view came into thcir reach (not excluding the sizable brown banderole with the design of a green maple leaf) because they were strolling towards it and sighting it from very faraway being following their leader.

A towering tower which had a mixture of pewter and ivory on its spruce walls, which stood at a distance of about forty-five metres from the school building on its left, it also had numerous floors. The entire area was enumerated as school property and was indeed a massive area to be under the jurisdiction of it. On the right of the school was an extensive conservatory with several uncanny floras inside it as being viewed by the students although it was closed. Masarah directed them to keep following her; instead of taking them to the edifice she took them to the tower.

The tower had a big entrance which looked patently splendid despite of the fact that it should have looked shabby as it was ramshackle (by appearance) and also as there was no adornment at all and to the top of all, the color (the color on the walls) choices were certainly irrelevant, it seemed as a novice was provided with the task but somehow it looked sterling spruce. The old lady ceased her strolling due to which one or two students had to make it back a few steps so as to prevent themselves from bumping onto the lady. She told them to drop their suitcases on the stoned floor of the tower and step backwards onto their positions, one by one they came and placed their suitcases as instructed. After that the old lady stepped forward, out emerged her hands and with a flick of a wave of her hands, all the bags began to flutter and began to go inside by airway "Masarah ! We've not been admitted yet !" The old lady and all the students turned their heads towards the voice, it had been said by Eveline. She said "The new students aren't needed to take admission in the month of May as this month is your trial month; you'll get yourselves introduced to the teachers as well as you'll get how they teach and if you like their method of teaching then in next month you can take admission and there's no fee required to be deposited for the trial month." The trio exchanged contented looks just as the other students did.

"Now you may head to your classrooms." Said Masarah loudly to everyone standing there, Sam asked getting nonplussed "Why do you suppose we'd be knowing our classrooms ? We haven't been there before." Masarah responded beamingly "Well, that's quite facile, you'll find listicles in the lobby, from which you'd enable yourselves to make it to your specific classes." All the students nodded and began to move in the queue without pushing one another though Masarah was left behind. They were strolling forward towards the school building which somewhat was extravagant to the students as they could no longer view the top although not all of the students had stopped themselves in tracks, many looked at the edifice as it was listless. The entrance was much more sizable than the tower's one, as the queue stepped in; they weren't flabbergasted to sight a long lobby with many rooms with laths on which grades were written; on the far left end was a staircase just like the right end although there were elevators too just adjacent to the staircase though at a distance. The students were not going to move and cease their gazing until the jet black-haired girl said out loud "Are we not supposed to look for the lists ?" Everyone nodded except for herself (obviously she would not nod on her own comment made for the others), it did not take any long for the triplets to find the lists whereas the others were still engaged in gaping. There were not numerous lists but were a few.

All the students began to look for their names in order to get which classroom they had been allotted with to carry on for the term, it was fortunate of the trio or as luck would have them, they did not get squashed or squeezed among the chaos as hustling as well as bustling carried on for next twenty minutes although the trio did not get chance to look over to the lists because of the rush. Finally when students began to move to the classrooms to which they were supposed to after gaping scrupulously on the lists with their fingers running through the labels. "Look here's yours !" Cried out Sam without even realizing that he was very much close to a little boy's ear who in return had yelled while splattering his spittle onto his shirt "Do you want me to be hearing-impaired ?!" Sam glared at him but Eveline stamped on his foot and apologized to the boy while blocking his mouth with her own hand, the boy smiled back to her cutely and rushed towards the elevator on the right. Eveline let go of Sam's maw and let him say "What do you think you've done ? Do you even know he was spitting onto me ?!" Eveline chuckled then said teasingly "Do you consider that little amount to be a million barrels ? Oh come on you didn't get drenched up, did you ?" Sam gave her a death-stare then said bitterly "Can you stay out of my business ? I'm not being necessitated to have you around me every so often dealing with me which would certainly be a ridiculous thing for a bookworm like you and also because I don't require you edifying me invariably." Eveline's eyes rolled onto him from the list as her own words made their way off her mouth "You cannot talk to me like that. And for your kind perusal, you were the one whose was being faulty to yowl in his ear like-" "I'm not being in the necessity of knowing that. And if you could assist me by being taciturn then it'll be great for sure and I'll be obliged if you could do so." Eveline's eyes were burning with rage, she wanted to speak but could not. Jim on the contrast was glancing over the list in order to turn a blind eye. He spoke up so as to suppress the quarrel "We better get going or else we'd be late, I've seen our names, we have to head to grade seven section B which is on the second floor." The two heard him but did not speak and began strolling forward together with the back of their heads facing one another's back of head. Jim followed them.

They made it to the escalator on the left via moving their legs and as soon as they entered it, they heard a virtual male's voice "Which floor are you intending to go to ?" The trio was stupefied but managed to say together "Second floor" in an ordinary voice although they pretended to be usual but were not, the escalator had begun to move upwards when the trio tried back to normal. Very soon they landed on the floor as the door fell open, the three strolled and were bewildered to see a corridor which looked exactly same as the lobby although the grades' panels had different grades which certainly indicated that it was another floor. The triplets strolled further, were mystified to hear not a single voice coming out of the classrooms, neither of the teacher's nor the students'; it seemed as though they were all deserted.

They allowed their legs to cease the strolling in front of a door with a panel on top 'Grade 7 Section – B' labeled onto it. As they were about to turn the doorknob it turned automatically which meant someone else was opening it from the other side, the three backed away in order not to bump onto that person and out emerged a girl of the same height as theirs, she had golden-brown curly hairs reaching up to her shoulders with a ebony colored plain hairband, her eyes seemed to be gorgeous enough to add up to her prettiness or it should be said her eyes were almost all of her beauty. She stood in their front and asked cheerfully "New students, right ?" The three nodded while gazing at her eyes, the girl said charmingly "Go inside then." As she completed saying she drifted into another class, the three watched her going.

The triplets made themselves to penetrate into the classroom where several students were already sitting chit-chatting with each other. The room had tidy walls with no scribbling at all (as the three's orphanage's classrooms had), the walls had a few charts stuck on them, one of them had variables, equations, mathematical formulae, identities, etc.. (They belonged to the subject – Mathematics), one of them had pictures of chemical compounds, elements, flora, fauna, microscopic organisms, physicists etc.. (They belonged to the subject – Science) and last one had pictures as well as names of some peculiar monuments, statues, woods, herbs-shrubs, water bodies etc.. (They belonged to the subject – General Magical Knowledge). On the left hand side of the trio were the benches with numerous children on the right hand side that was basically the front of the class was a polished desk as well as a polished wooden chair (a little bit bigger) was placed beside the big blackboard along with a small plank attached horizontally to the bottom's border of the blackboard so as to keep the duster and the colorful chalks, the classroom also had three-four medium sized windows and five-six fans fixed to the roof.

As the three made it to a vacant bench (which had the extent of holding four individuals) in the front, the eyes of many children drifted at them, all of them glanced at them scrupulously without blinking. The trio didn't react and silently got seated on the bench while plunking down their schoolbags.

"Hey Evans !" Out came a voice from their behind, Eveline quickly jerked her face to turn it at her back as she had heard a familiar voice and as she rolled her eyes she enabled them to view a very handsome figure sitting on the bench at her back in between a boy and a girl. "Hi Kevin ! How come you're here ? Wait are you also a student of this grade ?" The very handsome boy beamed while nodding, Eveline grinned and said delightedly "That's pretty great ! By the way did you get your books ?" Kevin responded charmingly "Yeah I did."

At that jiff, the boy sitting beside him murmured something into his ear which coerced him to say "Anyways Let me introduce to my buddies." Jim and Sam were quiet, Eveline glanced at the two partners of Kevin as he allowed his maw to say out to her "This is Adrien." He pointed his hand towards the black-haired, swollen lipped boy who wore spectacles, on his left hand side, the boy said uninterestedly "Hello, my name's Adrien Monton and yeah you can consider me to be reticent as I am." Eveline smiled and replied politely "Hi I am Eveline Guitonnet, nice to meet you." Kevin then gestured his hand towards the girl on his right and said cheerfully "And this is Naomi, another best friend of mine just like you." Eveline looked at the blonde-haired and red cheeked girl with a mole below her rose pink lips. The girl said confidently though uninterestedly "Hi ! I'm Naomi Fillurs. Nice to meet you !"

Eveline said happily "Nice to meet you too, Naomi." The jet black haired girl as well as boy began to converse earnestly.

"When the class is supposed to begin ?" Interrupted the dark blue-haired boy, Naomi answered unintentionally "At quarter to nine." Sam glimpsed at his bro's wristwatch which was striking half past eight as Jim while looking at Eveline and Kevin, questioned "What's the timetable ? Which class is supposed to be this one ?" Naomi glanced at him for a jiff then responded "We haven't got the timetable yet, we'll get it today as it's our very first class." Jim kept looking at the two while responding "Hmm, is that so ? Then we've to wait until the clock strikes 8:45, right ?" Naomi smirked and said "There's no option else than that."

Eveline and Kevin were gossiping eagerly about their holidays, while Jim was staring at them and Sam was gaping at his bro, after a while he whisperingly asked to him "Why are you constantly looking at them ?" Jim turned his head towards him and as he was about to say, the classroom door swung open.

The two boys looked, the same queen of beauty stepped in with a pile of books in her arms and her bag on her back; she strolled at the back of the classroom and put them on a desk, after which she took a gander of the entire class (it seemed as she was searching for something or somebody), her glimpsing came to a cease when she got a glance of the trio. She strolled towards their bench and as she reached, she asked in an appealing tone "May I sit with you three ?" This time Eveline too had her head towards her. The trio replied together "Of course, there's no problem at all." She sat beside Jim as she plunked down her bag.

"Hi myself Tulip Albatross !" Said the girl cheerfully as a hand of hers erupted to do handshake with the dark blue-haired boy, Jim without any hesitation did the handshake and said charmingly "Hi ! My name is Jim Sueruds, nice to meet you !" The girl replied delightedly "Nice to meet you too ! And what's your good name ?" She looked at Sam, he responded without any delay "I'm Sam Mahongthan, nice to meet you, Tulip." The girl nodded happily, then she peered at Eveline who was busily conversing with Kevin. She said to her "And what's your name ?" Eveline didn't hear her that is why she kept going on with her conversation, Tulip found it a bit weird, then Jim said to her "She's our friend Eveline Guitonnet." Tulip glanced at him then said "Hmm, well anyways I think you three are the only new ones in our class." Sam said "Is that so ?" The girl nodded in affirmative as she heard him. "By the way where do you live in MMW ?" Asked Tulip cheerfully to the two boys, Sam answered as he saw Jim gaping at Eveline and Kevin "Actually we're not only just new to this class but are also new to this magical world." The girl widened her eyes, then said "Oh, then I think you people would be under the action of the survival incantation, right ?" Sam replied "Yes we are, by the way are you a native citizen ?" Tulip nodded then poked Jim on his elbow which he took a bit uncanny then he asked "What ?" The girl asked enthusiastically "How does it feel like being bounded by the survival charm ?" Jim and Sam exchanged weird looks with one another then Jim said "It feels ordinary." Tulip asked getting nonplussed "Something must be different, I mean you might feel a bit or even much more than a bit vigorous or something like that, don't you feel ?" Jim answered straight forwardly "No it doesn't feel like that. Nothing has changed, we feel like we did before." Sam also made his maw to let off "Yup no changes."

Eveline was still conversing with Kevin which was very much listless as well as provoking to Adrien and Naomi as

Eveline was not letting them speak a word to their best friend. On the other hand Tulip made a profound bond of friendship with the two boys by continuously gossiping with them.

After a while every student had to turn silent and to get to their feet as the door unclosed, a plump physique entered, some students at the back had also mumbled "Good morning soccer ball" But the man had not heard them although the trio did hear and Eveline did say slowly "How ruthless of them ! They're body-shaming him !" The boys did not say anything but Tulip did say "Yes they're habitual of this." Eveline looked at her and said slowly and happily "I'm Eve-" "I know that they told me, but you won't be knowing me, I'm Tulip Albatross." Eveline widened up her eyes and was about to say something when many students got off their seats and made it to the teacher's desk; the students took off chocolates, wafers, presents etc.. and put them on the man's desk, he seemed very much pleased as he said "Thank you so much, my darlings !" The students beamed and headed back to their benches.

"Does he educate up to the mark ?" Asked Sam to Tulip, she without looking at him responded "Na.. not very finely, I think moderate." "Then what's the reason behind getting ample number of gifts ?" Asked Jim confusedly "Well it's like this, he's not a fair person as he's always demanding for presents and other entertainment stuff from his favorite students." Answered she while taking out her hefty book, following Eveline.

"Good Morning My Darlings ! I hope all of you had had a great time with your families but now as you can see the vacations are no longer here for you. The old students as well as new students I'd like to tell you this that I'll be your class teacher for this entire year for sure. And I also wanna tell you that you're gonna be fond of my classes-" "Fib" Mumbled Tulip, the boys heard her and giggled whereas Eveline didn't react at all. "So before beginning the class you all would be expecting me to tell the timetable, so let me get to your expectation. Here let you note the timetable I'm dictating." The students took out their rough copies as well as their pens and were ready.

"First period will be taken by me, for the new students let me introduce myself to themselves. So I am Adam Se Johnson, your General Magical Knowledge's professor." Said the plump physique loudly for everyone to hear. The students' pens began to commit to paper. "The second period will be taken by Mister Kim Tao Zenchan and it'll be your Science class for certain." Jim beamed at hearing that, being a science lover. The students jotted down quickly as being told, "Third period is of Mathematics which will be taken by Miss Intiana Kimtriger." The students noted down once again, this time Eveline grinned as Mathematics was her favorite subject, Tulip noticed that. "Fourth period will be taken by Mister Milkan Mator who will be your professor for Social Studies." Jim and Sam jotted it down sorrowfully as they hated Social Studies whereas Tulip looked very happy when she was being asked by Jim about the reason, she told him that social studies was her favorite subject. "After the fourth period you'll be having your recess of half an hour, then after it will be your fifth period which will be of Common Operating Machine Purposely Used for Technological and Educational Research, I hope you got it." The students glanced at him mystifyingly, that was when Eveline & Tulip said out loud "It's Computer." Everybody looked at the girls including the professor. He said "Yes obviously, very well said !" Jim patted at Eveline's back.

"And the last period will be taken by Stanklin Samthon who will be your professor for English." Said the man while unclosing a packet of chips and a chocolate, he inserted a handful of chips and a dark chocolate into his mouth in one go. "Disgusting !" Cried out many girls including Tulip and Eveline. Whereas the boys just stared at the treats as they drooled excluding Jim and Kevin.

As the disgusting professor of theirs swallowed the mixture, he allowed himself to have another chocolate and while stuffing it into is maw, he began to say cheerfully "Now let you move to page number three chapter number one 'THE IMPLAUSIBLE FLORA' and have a look at the topic number one 'Glorie Morie'." Every student did as told.

"So first of all, if anyone knows about the topic, what is 'Glorie Morie' in actual ?" Asked the professor as he leaped to his feet, lifted his hands up in the air, fidgeted his right hand in a peculiar manner (just as he was holding a small cylindrical object while fluttering his left hand at the holder at the bottom of the blank blackboard; the trio had their eyes on their professor marvelously; one of the chalks raised up to a level of the professor's left hand, he moved his left hand towards his right one and the chalk fluttered towards his right hand which was already in a position of holding it. The professor scribbled on the neat blackboard '**THE IMPLAUSIBLE FLORA**' and below it '**NUMBER ONE - Glorie Morie**'. As the man turned he saw only two hands striking the air particles, he knew whose was one of them but he wasn't aware of the second one as he lowered his sight he got to see a jet black-haired beautiful girl. He said to that girl while glancing at her "Yes you may tell me." Eveline stood up confidently and answered "'Glorie Morie' is the most venomous parasitic plant found in the north-eastern parts of MMW's one of the densest forests 'Luang

Katira', it is medium-heighted and possesses a length of approximately fifteen centimetres, sometimes due to extra nutrition it could also reach up to eighteen centimetres." Finished the smart girl "Excellent !" The man praised as he clapped his hands together.

"Your name my darling ?" Asked he impressively to her, "Eveline Guitonnet" She replied politely with a little smile on her pretty face "Miss Guitonnet, very well explained. You're absolutely correct." The man appreciated again as she sat back. "So according to miss Guitonnet's correct explanation, 'Glorie Morie' is the most poisonous freeloading plant but do you people know what's very noteworthy about it ?" Asked the professor, again two arms were up in the air. Jim and Sam being knowing their best friend, were aware of her splendid memory, the doublets knew that she would have read the book at nights in their stay at her uncle's flat. "Yes miss Guitonnet" The man asked, Tulip shook her hand as well as head down. Jim noticed Tulip and while feeling bad for her he mumbled to himself "He should give a chance to her too."

"It has two very exceptional characteristics, number one is that it glows luminously once in a week and second is that it emits a sweet smell whenever it finds a jeopardous creature around itself, pushing itself more into jeopardy by doing so." Said Eveline confidently, the professor applauded then said "So as miss Guitonnet explained two most important fortes of the plant, so let me clarify it a bit more. Actually 'Glorie Morie' acquires its nutrition once in a week as it doesn't need more than that, that is why it emits light just like a luminous object in order to attract its prey." The man took a pause, stepped towards his desk, picked up a chocolate, broke it into two halves and began gobbling up the first half. The students watched him devouringly except for some.

"Now who'll describe it's structure ?" Asked the professor while tending to slobber although he stroked his tongue over the mixture of his own saliva and melted chocolate dripping down his chin. Numerous students threw him looks of repugnance as they prevented their eyes from watching the boorish man. This time Eveline also had her eyes off the man although her hand had struck the air molecules swiftly as the professor's words made their way from his maw to the exquisite girl's ears, Tulip's arm was also up in the air and she very much eager to answer the question but once again the discourteous professor handed the opportunity to her competitor.

"It somewhat looks like a popsicle, a green lean beanpole in the lower portion and an amber colored round ball on its top along with some little sterling white bulbs." Answered the pretty girl confidently, whereas Jim and Sam glanced at the hapless and sorrowed competitor of hers. "Very good my darling !" Exclaimed the chubby man without glancing at her. "Now although it looks like a popsicle but if you go on to intake it then certainly you won't find yourself in a fine fettle afterwards and I'd patently not suggest you to do so, as an alternative I'd suggest you to purchase a real popsicle or perhaps more than one in order to hand the others to me as you won't like to have it without handling one to me being your most beloved professor." The professor finished beamingly, his best-loved students did grin but several did not including the dark blue-haired boy, the grey-haired boy, the jet black haired girl, the curly golden-brown haired girl, the jet black haired boy, the blonde-haired girl and the swollen-lipped boy (overall the front benchers as well as the second-front benchers).

"Very well, now who will tell me a very significant fact about 'Glorie Morie' ?" Asked the professor, once again two hands were striking the air. This opportunity was also provided to Eveline, but as she was going to respond, she was being interrupted by Tulip who yowled in rage "Sir I am also present here and am constantly raising my hand ! Why aren't you giving a single opportunity of answering to me ?!" "Miss Albatross ! You aren't supposed to holler like that ! And about the stuff that you prattled off your filthy mouth right away, then I think you should also provide chances to others ! Now sit down !" Yelled the professor without glimpsing at her, Tulip fell silent although her eyes did not stay quiet as they were bulging with sparkling pearls of rage and insult, Sam and Jim began to console her.

Eveline took a glimpse of the offended exquisite girl and as she took her own eyes off her she began "I guess the most important fact about the plant is that once it was being utilized by the most renowned witch christened as 'Sarah Bones' so as to conquer over gaiety." The professor clapped his hands and appreciated "Excellent my darling ! Very well !" Then the man seated himself back to his wooden chair and responded with satisfaction in his voice "Very well, here half of your topic finishes and now you may relax as I guess there're numerous jiffs with which you're left to spend with me. And I'm very much aware of the fact that you no longer possess the enthusiasm of getting more things into your brain therefore now you may sit and stay quiet until the period gets over though you can converse with one another." All the students glanced at him rapidly, their eyes were like a ricocheting bullet, this was very much appalling to them as they had just begun and half of the topic was done. Many students at the back mumbled "What a speed this soccer ball possesses !" This time Eveline did not hear them haply.

The professor began to demolish the wafers with his fists after which he crammed them into his maw. The girls watched him with utter revulsion just like the boys.

Kevin and Eveline began to converse with another once again as they'd got the chance to do so whereas Jim and Sam gazed at Tulip whose cheeks were still damp, the two being gentlemen decided to entail her words in their riveting discussion of 'The history of MMW'.

"So this world was be extant from a prolonged duration of time, right ?" Asked the handsome dark blue-haired boy to Tulip to which she responded with a counterfeit grin "Yeah and from that very jiff OMSOM had also been here." Sam asked astoundingly "What d'you mean by the very jiff ? How could it be in extant from the very jiff as it must be erected by an organization or somebody, mustn't it ?" Tulip responded beamingly "Yup it was constructed by someone." "Who if you know ?" Asked Jim queerly while glancing at Eveline and Kevin who were laughing heartily, he wondered what they were talking about as neither he nor Sam were able to catch their words. Not just because they didn't intend to do so but also because the two gigglers also weren't in the intention of letting anybody hear them.

As the doublets perceived the two laughers to laugh even more cordially than before, they allowed their nosiness to intensify. Now they weren't paying attention to Tulip despite they wanted to get to know about the matter which was a matter of guffawing.

"Hey ! Are you two listening ?" Asked out a voice, the two had to jerk their heads towards the prettiest girl over there, "Yes ! Yes we are, Tulip." Said the two boys at once as they got it back into their respective minds what they were supposed to do and what not. "Are you two jealous of him ?" Asked Tulip as she smirked. The two boys replied swiftly along with their cheeks getting scarlet "Of course not ! We are just curious about the topic !" Tulip asked while looking away "Doesn't seem like." Jim responded "To you but the truth is we aren't envious at all and it's kind of eccentric to converse for so long on a matter persistently without paying attention to others, therefore we're just a bit inquisitive after all it is an ordinary idiosyncrasy, isn't it ?" Tulip nodded with utter certitude while staring at Eveline through the corners of her eyes. Sam asked "Anyways what were you saying ?" Tulip responded "Well, we were talking bout who had erected this building." Jim asked swiftly "Yeah so who had ?" Tulip answered "Well, you must have got to sight the a tall tower that's nearly forty-five metres away this school building, right ?" The boys nodded as they heard her. Tulip continued "So that tower was once the school building, this building was not being constructed until then but later on when this got erected, this was declared as the school building and from then onwards we got to study here only." The boys hummed and asked together "So it means that tower which will serve as a hostel was first erected ?" Tulip nodded with a genuine smile on her face then she continued "If I talk about the person who constructed the tower and the school building, then he is the same individual; our superintendent." Jim asked "And who's he ?"

"Sir Rason" Tulip responded in an esteemed as well as overwhelmed voice.

**TO BE CONTINUED..**